Adventures in the Neighborhood Woods
The Tunnel

Adventures in the Neighborhood Woods

The Tunnel

By Jesse Honn

Edited by Phil Honn and Jesse Honn
Published by Life Flight Media™, LLC
Sand Springs, Oklahoma
www.LifeFlightMedia.com

Adventures in the Neighborhood Woods
The Tunnel
By Jesse Honn

Part of the *Adventures in the Neighborhood Woods*™ series.

This book is a fictional work. All characters, places, events, and names are used fictitiously for the purpose of entertainment. Real-world resemblances, if any, are coincidental.

Published by Life Flight Media™, LLC
21503 West 71st Street South
Sand Springs, Oklahoma 74063-6448
www.LifeFlightMedia.com

Author: Jesse Honn
Executive Editor: Phil Honn
Editor: Jesse Honn
Design, Layout, Photos: Jesse Honn
Proofreading: Jennifer Honn

First edition published 2009.

Printed in the United States of America
15 14 13 12 11 10 09 1 2 3 4 5

Library of Congress Control Number: 2009908262
ISBN-13: 978-0-9823899-2-8 (PAPERBACK)
ISBN-10: 0-9823899-2-2 (PAPERBACK)

Introducing a New Series for Kids

Life Flight Media is introducing the *Adventures in the Neighborhood Woods* series of adventure books for ages 8+ (eight and up) for anyone who loves a fun, clean, fascinating tale of discovery, mystery, and friendship.

The *Adventures in the Neighborhood Woods* series follows the exploits of regular kids who somehow find their way into extraordinary situations. These kids are like any other kids. They do schoolwork, complete their chores, play games, meet with friends, and have both problems and successes just like any other kids. However, these kids love a good adventure, and they are daring enough to explore deep within the neighborhood woods and ultimately the greater world beyond the neighborhood. Follow them as they learn about adventure, nature, friendship, and life.

When you want the kind of exciting adventures like only kids could have, look for the following logo:

Adventures in the Neighborhood Woods

CONTENTS

Chapter 1
Summer Party

Dace awoke to the soft chirping of a cricket outside his window. The sun had just begun to peek into his room, casting everything in a pleasant, soft glow. The clock displayed 6:39. Dace wasn't used to waking so early, but he knew this was an important week. It was the last week of school before summer break!

Quickly, Dace ripped away the chocolate-brown bed cover and wriggled out of his video game sheets. His feet hit the floor running as he rushed to the shower. It was time to get an early jump on his schoolwork. Dace was homeschooled, and if he could just finish two days of work today and two days of work tomorrow, he could finish his last day of work on Wednesday. Then he would be out for the summer! Dace was sure his mom would approve and let him out a couple days early as long as all of his work was done. He had important things to do later that week.

Steam filled the air and bubbles flew as Dace vigorously scrubbed himself clean, during which time he thought through the week's plans more thoroughly. As refreshing as the shower was, he was eager to complete his next morning step: breakfast.

Ah, breakfast time. Wonderful, scrumptious breakfast! Dace always thought he made the best breakfast and so did his family. Every few weeks, he loved to get up early and surprise his mom with a delicious breakfast of eggs, hash browns, cinnamon toast, and, of course, orange juice *plus* milk (in separate cups, usually!). He just *had* to have milk in the morning. It went down great with waffles, cinnamon toast, pancakes, strawberries, and nearly anything truly worth eating. Milk was Dace's drink of choice.

With his shower completed, Dace devoured his breakfast. This morning there wasn't going to be a big spread ready for the family to eat. He was in a hurry, so cereal was his consolation prize. At least it was the type of crunchy sweetness that gave him a burst of energy that lasted just long enough before lunchtime. However, he needed his brain to be on its best behavior today, so he figured he ought to eat some fruit for good measure. A pear and an apple later and Dace had finished his breakfast.

7:15. Dace had completed his morning rituals in record time and began his first subject: spelling. He was good at spelling. He always thought it was the easiest subject, so he did it first. Words came easily to Dace. He may have been a better writer than speaker, but he could go on and on for hours about almost anything. Spelling and language were his favorite subjects aside from art. This morning he'd be doing twice as much spelling as usual, but that wouldn't take long. A little while later he had moved on to language, then math, then science. And so it went throughout the morning.

Around 10:30, Dace's mother, Beverly, checked in on him because he'd been unusually quiet this morning. He laid out his plans for an early end to the school year, and she approved, although with the stipulation that he do top-notch work. Sloppiness wasn't allowed. After all, the point of schoolwork was to learn something. Dace agreed with a nod of his head and a grunt as he continued writing something scientific in his notebook.

When lunchtime rolled around, Dace had completed nearly two days of schoolwork in record time. He had just another hour or so to go before he was done for the day.

As he chewed on an egg salad sandwich, he went over his plans for the weekend. His best friend, Jeff, who went to the school across the street from Dace's house, finished the school year on Thursday. His other pals, Nao, Donovan (simply called "Van" by his friends), and Leila, were all homeschooled. They each expected to finish the school year at the end of the week.

Dace and Jeff were planning a big "Summer's Starting!" party Friday night, then everyone was going to play games all day Saturday. On Sunday, Dace's family would be going to their yearly family reunion which traditionally took place the day before Memorial Day. Then the big day would be upon them. On Memorial Day (Monday), Dace and his friends planned to spend the whole day in the woods, mapping and searching for answers to the secrets buried within. They'd been talking about it for weeks.

Dace's mother had some errands to run on Tuesday, so Dace only completed one day of schoolwork that day. He hated to fall behind, but he remembered to pick up some supplies for the weekend. The day wasn't a total loss, after all. Dace was now on track to finish on Thursday. Finally on Thursday at 2:38 p.m., Dace was officially out of school for the summer.

Summertime! It was equated in Dace's mind with fun and adventure. It was that beautiful time of year when the imagination could run wild and everyone felt a little more free than usual. Parents even seemed more lenient and relaxed, and every kid knew that meant things could get interesting quickly. Fun was lurking around every corner. There would be barbeques, games, friends, family get-togethers, swimming pools, amusement parks—the possibilities were endless. Let the adventures begin!

Around four o'clock, the phone rang. It was Jeff calling for Dace. As Dace rushed to the phone, he anticipated Jeff's next move. Jeff was supposed to have asked his mom if he could spend the night at Dace's that night.

Jeff's sly voice was heard on the phone. "Uh, Dace, I have some bad news. My mom is sick, and she said I'm going to have to stay home this weekend."

"What!" Dace exclaimed unbelievingly. They had been planning the big Friday night party and adventure in the woods on Monday for months! Everyone knew that this would be the biggest bash of the year. After all, it was the beginning of summer break! Why couldn't Jeff's mom be sick some other time? Dace thought parents always had a way of changing their kid's plans at the last second, just when everything was about to go through smoothly.

"Gotcha!" Jeff laughed. "My mom said I have to mow the yard first and do a few chores, but I can come over afterwards. Umm, I could get it done a lot faster with some help. Do you mind helping?"

"Sure. Let's do it fast, though. We have preparations to do for the party tomorrow," Dace replied hurriedly.

The walk to Jeff's house was only a few blocks, but Dace was in a hurry, so he ran. By the time he arrived, he was out of breath but happy because he had beat Jeff's fastest time! They had an ongoing race to see who could get to the other's house the quickest. There were times for running, walking, riding a bike, and, oddly enough, riding a skateboard even though neither of them could really ride one without bloodying their hands on the sidewalk at some point. One time they even considered adding a fastest time for riding an animal, but neither of them could figure out how to do it without getting in trouble. They had considered lassoing a neighbor's Great Dane, but that didn't seem right. In any case, Dace was now the fastest runner.

As soon as Dace was thinking that the early evening summer sun warming his back was one of the best feelings in the world, the chores were complete. The yard was freshly mowed (although it looked a bit too short because

Jeff didn't want to have to mow again for a while), the trash was sitting at the curb for a smelly Friday morning pickup, and Jeff's room appeared to be clean enough. There was still a strange smell coming out from under the bed somewhere, but that could wait for later. It was time for summer to begin in earnest.

Jeff rode his bike as Dace walked back to get his from the garage at home. Dace hadn't ridden his bike to Jeff's earlier in the evening because getting the bike out of the garage was always a long adventure in itself. It usually involved climbing over random pieces of junk, squeezing around decades-old piles of boxes, and finally lifting his bike over his head and slowly making his way to the door. More than once Dace stubbed his toe or tripped and smashed his head in the process. Luckily at times his bike was already at the front of the garage near the door, but he never knew if that would be the case next time. Things had a way of mysteriously moving around, and no one ever knew how it happened.

As Jeff and Dace rode around the neighborhood, they discussed the next evening's party. There just *had* to be pizza at the party. Dace figured his mom could make her famous homemade pizzas that everyone loved so much. The crust was so fluffy, and the sauce was so saucy! There was never-ending cheese piled high. Pepperonis, olives, and mushrooms were always generously strewn about, just the way Dace liked it. Dace used to not like mushrooms, but he'd tried them one time when he and his friends had started a short-lived video game club. Club members were supposed to eat some mushrooms as a tribute to their favorite mushroom-loving video game plumber, and now pizza just wasn't pizza without a few mushrooms.

The two friends also discussed who was coming to the party. Jeff's younger brother, Kevin, would be coming, along with Dace's longtime homeschooling friend, Nao, and his two younger brothers. Of course only the older guys were going to spend the night. The little kids had to go back home later in the evening. Dace and Jeff's other friend, Van, would be there as well. Leila, a girl Dace sometimes met with for a few homeschooling lessons each month, would also be there. All in all, the party was shaping up to be a ton of fun and a great beginning to summer.

The next evening, people began to arrive at Dace's house for the party. The first order of business was, of course, to hold a video game competition. There were five different games in various categories, and the competition was wild! At first Dace and Van, the two self-proclaimed video game masters, were tied for first place with wins at racing, platform jumping, and sports games. Ultimately though, Leila surprised everyone with her huge score at boxing, and she eventually won first place after dealing a defeating blow to Van. Suddenly, everyone realized they were hungry; then it was off to the kitchen for pizza.

"I love your mom's pizza! I wish my mom made it like this," Leila said as she tore into her third slice. "We should have this again on Monday."

"Ah, yes. Monday!" Dace said excitedly. "Is everybody going to be able to come? We have a job for each person to do. This year is the year we conquer the woods," he proclaimed as everyone munched on cheese and pepperoni.

"I think I can bring my dad's metal detector," Jeff said tentatively.

Then Nao spoke up with important news. "My parents said I could use the GPS device if I promise to be careful with it. We'll be able to trace our path through the woods. Maybe we could bury a time capsule or something and record the location for the future."

"That'd be *awesome*!" Dace slurred with a full mouth. "We should all find some stuff this weekend to put in a box and make a time capsule."

Everyone agreed the time capsule would be a cool idea. As the conversation continued, someone mentioned snakes. Poisonous snakes. The woods were teeming with them this time of year (at least everyone seemed to think so). There were poisonous rattlesnakes, copperheads, cottonmouths, and surely some other super-ultra-death snakes! Just then Dace's dad, Tom, got home from arguing another court case at work and overheard the snake talk. He assured the kids that there were very few snakes around, even though a few of the poisonous ones did live in that area. Dace and his friends seemed to feel a little better about it, but they secretly planned to take some weapons, just in case. They'd have to work on those weapons sometime before Monday, and Nao said they could probably use his garage and his dad's tools for the job. Van mentioned that he had some extra metal lying around that was left over from his parent's last home renovation project. Surely they could make something useful from that.

Dace's mom surprised everyone after the meal by announcing that she had rented the latest science-fiction movie, *Space Attack Dingbats*, for the group to watch if they wanted. Everyone enthusiastically agreed to watch it. Later on when the moles were done beaming down from space and clawing their way through the earth's crust (and the humans somehow survived to live another day), it was time for the younger kids and Leila to go home. Jeff, Nao, and Van stayed the night.

That night as Jeff had just reached level twelve on his adventure game, he had an interesting thought. What if, just like in the level eleven sacred woods challenge, there were hidden passageways in the real woods? Wouldn't it be neat if they could find something in the woods that no one else had ever found before? Maybe there was something that had been hidden away throughout out time, only to be unearthed by them for the first time ever. Surely with all of their gadgets, brainpower, and knack for solving mysteries, they could uncover the secrets of those woods. Maybe this would be the year. Maybe *this summer* would be the best summer yet!

Chapter 2
Enter the Woods

On Sunday, Dace and his family went to the park for their yearly family reunion. Dace loved the family reunion because there was usually great weather outside, many activities for the kids to do, and a bunch of interesting foods that he only got to try once a year. Sometimes Dace and his cousins went fishing and looked for strange little creatures in the shallows of the stream. They often found crawfish hiding under rocks, and one time Dace found a miniature baby turtle (a red-eared slider, he thought). There were sometimes giant bullfrog tadpoles to be found hiding in the shallows. Yes, the family reunion was a great beginning to summer vacation.

Dace found his cousin, Anthony, lounging around the desserts. As Anthony plopped a huge piece of Aunt Marge's cherry cake onto his stars-and-stripes-themed plate, Dace laughed and quipped, "You gonna leave any of that for anyone else?"

"I would, but I'm trying to save everyone else all of those calories. I'm doing my duty to protect the health of the food-eating public!" Anthony replied.

Dace continued the banter. "I bet you're morally obligated to eat that whole gallon of ice cream as well. And, of course, you'll need a two-liter of Sugar Dew soda to wash it all down."

Not fazed, Anthony whipped back, "Oh, I'd love to, but I think your momma already ate all of the ice cream!"

Although continuing their yearly game would have been fun, Dace decided there were more important matters to discuss. He was ready to get down to business. In a hushed voice he said, “Hey, let’s go somewhere we can talk in private. There’s something big we have to discuss.”

The old evergreen tree behind the baseball field provided perfect cover for their covert operations. That tree had seen a million secret meetings and shady deals. Every kid knew that the imposing tree was the place to go when you didn’t want your parents to know what was going on. It was now time to discuss the important gear for tomorrow’s big adventure.

Dace began the meeting. “My friend, Van, said he has some metal that we can make some weapons from. We’re going to Nao’s garage tonight to work on them. My mom said we can stay the night at Nao’s house, so no one will worry about what we’re doing tonight. We’ve got to protect ourselves out there in the woods. Who knows what could be out there. I’ve even heard there are mountain lions or something.”

And to a point, Dace was right about the dangerous woods. There were untold hazards far beyond simple rattlesnakes lurking in the woods. The only problem was that crude weapons wouldn’t be enough to protect them from what the woods held. Adventure—and danger—was hiding in every nook, every cranny, and every dark place that beckoned the gang to those mysterious woods. Those ancient rocks, rippling streams, and towering trees knew more of human existence than all the historians and scientists could ever hope to uncover. A peek into those mysteries was waiting for anyone brave enough to venture within the woods.

Anthony seemed a bit worried about the danger, but he only spoke of the need for weapons as well as defensive items. “Weapons are good, I guess, but what do we have for defense? Also, what about stuff lik aid, and the all-important snacks?"

"Don't worry; we've got it covered. Leila' nging all of the snacks, Van said he has some protective gear, and I'm a trained first-aid specialist, remember. No problems!" Dace expressed his confidence, but Anthony wasn't totally convinced.

As the sun's light slowly faded into a dark-blue sky warmed by the glow of the city lights, the family reunion slowly came to an end. Anthony was going to spend the week with Dace, so the two went home together and prepared to make weapons that night.

Later in Nao's garage, Dace, Anthony, Nao, and Van tried to make a slingshot and a few swords. None of the weapons were particularly practical for their intended purposes, but they looked really cool. Anthony also made a wooden shield because he thought they didn't have enough defensive tools. Everyone laughed when Van suggested they try to make a hot air balloon to scout out the woods from above. They even tried filling a small balloon with hot air, but they somehow ended up catching it on fire and had to temporarily evacuate the garage. In the end, they had three dull but awesome-looking swords, some dowels attached together with screws in a Y shape, and a wooden shield emblazoned with a fireball on the front.

Nao had an idea. "Hey, we need some sort of symbol to represent our journey. All of the great adventurers always had a symbol."

The others weren't sure about that, but they decided that the fireball on the shield would be their official symbol. They also came up with a name for their group: The Woodsmen. Leila might not like it, but they figured she wouldn't mind once they told her that she'd been elected as group captain for the day's adventure. She had always been a born leader.

The next morning, everyone awoke early and rushed over to Dace's house after eating a filling breakfast of pancakes, sausages, and leftover chili with extra hot sauce. Leila was already there waiting for them, and Jeff arrived about twenty minutes later. After filling their water bottles and making sure all of their supplies were in order, The Woodsmen set off toward the woods as Dace's mom called behind them not to get into any trouble. She also reminded them to eat and drink lots of water during their adventures. Mothers are funny like that.

Actually, just before starting out, the boys let loose with their group name and symbol. Jeff thought the fireball symbol was awesome, and Leila didn't really mind the name once she learned that she was the group leader. "Well, just leader for the day," Van reminded her. Leila had longer-term plans for that, however.

The neighborhood woods were pretty close to Dace's house, but getting there involved a bit of work. The entrance (if one could call it that) to the woods was about a neighborhood block away. The only problem was that the gang had to walk through multiple backyards, cross a stream, and go through some high grass before they got there. Last year Dace and Jeff had built a small, wooden bridge across the stream. It worked great for a while, but they had forgotten to use treated wood which wouldn't rot, so the bridge had quickly fallen into disrepair. The best way to get across the stream now was to run and jump as fast as one could. That usually worked, but today Dace slipped at the last second and soaked his right leg in the cool water. He was angry for about half a second until he realized that it actually felt pretty good in the warm morning sun. He then proceeded to dip his other leg in the water for good measure.

After quickly slipping through a few backyards and hacking their way though many unkempt weeds, they approached the entrance to the woods and stopped to examine their adversary. The woods looked menacing upon first glance. The thick woods sat in a narrow valley between two steep, rocky cliffs on either side. The cliffs were twenty or thirty feet high in most places, and steep paths wound through the rocks in a few spots. There were thorny vines gnarled about every surface, and thick underbrush coated the damp ground. A stream ran through the middle of the valley, bringing needed water to the dense, tree-and-bush growth. Bugs crawled, slithered, inched, and flew just about everywhere, but they weren't so thick as to be overly annoying. In any case, the woods were a challenging and intimidating place, both physically and mentally.

The actual entrance to the woods was simple enough. There was an empty field far behind one of the neighborhood houses, and the stream provided a narrow, clear passageway into the dense growth. The group members looked at each other ominously and began to carefully squeeze their way into the opening at the edges of the water.

The first challenge was apparent immediately. Unless one wanted to walk in the middle of the stream, the dense brush would have to be sliced and hacked through to make a useable path. Luckily, some of the group carried swords that had been made the night before, and Dace had his dad's orange-handled machete, although it had a rather dull edge just like the swords. It was going to be slow traveling for now. No one in the group seemed to mind; they were having too much fun exploring the wonders of the woods.

Leila noticed a small, slender lizard with white stripes on its back. Van tried to catch it so they could examine the beast, but it was way too quick for the lumbering humans. Everyone got in on the action as they dived this way and that, grabbing for the lizard. Out of breath and a little scratched up by the thorny vines, the group finally gave up on lizard hunting, even though Dace really wanted a pet lizard to take home.

Leila spoke up and made her first decision as group leader. "I think we should stop for a few minutes and take a break. There is a small clearing behind those vines over there, and it looks like we can sit down on the rocks near the base of the cliff." No one disagreed with her pronouncement, so the group hacked its way over to the side of the narrow valley and into the small clearing.

Finding a clearing in the middle of dense woods was always an amazing thing. Entering in was like going inside a house without a roof. All around, dense walls of vegetation provided cover, but the sky up above was blue. The sun also shone brightly once again. There was a strange calmness about the clearing. The enterprising Woodsmen couldn't find anything unusual about it, but something seemed artificial about this clearing.

The first clue was a smell coming from somewhere near the rocky face of the cliff. Nao investigated and found a pile of rotting trash, a few old tires, and a rusted washing machine. The ground in the middle of the clearing was also charred black in a ten-foot-wide circle. Using their powers of deduction, the gang decided that one of the neighborhood houses on top of the cliff (for the neighborhood towered above the woods nestled in the valley below) must use this small clearing as a place to burn trash and discard old junk. It wasn't particularly exciting, but they had made their first discovery of the woods' many secrets.

As they sat drinking water and resting for a moment, a hawk was lazily circling high up in the sky. It seemed to be watching them, taking note of their covert movements within the woods. Dace wondered if the hawk was making plans to foil their great adventure. Maybe the hawk was actually recording everything to report back to his evil master hidden somewhere within the dark recesses of the woods. The master would gain a distinct advantage over the group by having his hawk give him regular reports. He could be planning the group's demise at that very moment, hoping to catch them off guard. If the gang got too close to his lair, he could strike like a snake hiding under the leaves, coiled and ready.

Snakes! The group was so busy relaxing and watching the hawk, they forgot about snakes! What if the rocks held countless rattlers or copperheads, just waiting for the right moment to sink their fangs into the juicy flesh of an adventurer? What if a band of nefarious cottonmouths was slithering its way silently down the stream, waiting for an errant foot to pass by? They were surrounded by poisons, fangs, and death! Suddenly, as if it knew what the gang was thinking at that moment, something darted out of the underbrush and went straight toward Nao, who was still over near the trash heap. Nao jumped back and yelped (a bit girlishly, Jeff thought) and began running toward the other side of the clearing. Nao's actions convinced the rest of the group to spring up and take flight as well. They all darted here and there about the clearing, running from a black blur of... whatever it was that was attacking them.

Someone screamed. It was Van, who, in all of the commotion, had cut his hand on a thorn. Dace and Jeff grabbed him and continued out of the clearing while hacking their way through the dense brush. Everyone was running and clawing their way aimlessly to somewhere else. Anywhere but where the attacker was mounting its wild rampage against the intruders.

As they madly forced their way deeper into the woods, Leila's cool head prevailed again. "Stop! Everybody stop!" she calmly but loudly declared.

That got everyone's attention, and they all came to a halt on the muddy, leaf-covered ground. No one knew how far they had run, but it surely couldn't have been far. How long had they been running? It was probably only a matter of ten or twenty seconds.

"Is everyone okay?" Leila asked. She surveyed the damage as each person nodded yes somewhat unenthusiastically. Van's hand was bleeding slightly, but it wasn't too bad. Dace already started to work on the hand and repair the damage as best as he could. Everyone else seemed fine.

"What *was* that thing?" Nao asked nervously. "I thought it was coming right for me. That thing moved a lot faster than any snake I ever saw before. I think it had fangs or large teeth in the front. It was trying to bite me!"

As Nao spoke, a small, black rabbit hopped toward the group. It stopped about ten feet away, still partly hidden in the brush. Everyone heard the rustling and looked over toward the rabbit. Nao had an embarrassed and somewhat horrified look on his face as he realized that he was staring directly into the eyes of his menacing adversary. A rabbit! A furry, cuddly, fluffy little rabbit! Van, forgetting the pain in his hand for the moment, started to laugh. A few seconds later and everyone was laughing hysterically. The bunny sat there staring at the group with innocent eyes. With a twitch of its nose, the rabbit casually turned toward the stream and hopped over for a quick drink.

"Forget about snakes. We've just met the biggest, most evil monster in the woods! Let's call him 'Slasher,'" quipped Van.

Everyone laughed at the irony of the situation. Here they were worried about snakes and evil hawk masters lurking within the woods, and they'd just adopted a new pet rabbit named Slasher. They knew they could count on him to protect them from whatever they might encounter. For it was the unknown, the dark crevices yet unexplored, to which they were going. They only had to plunge ahead into those dense woods to make history.

Chapter 3
Deeper into the Woods

While the group stood in the thicket deciding what to do next, Nao remembered the GPS device. He pulled it out of his backpack and started it up. He had meant to turn on its tracking feature in order to see where their adventures had led them, but he had forgotten. After a few minutes of fiddling with the device, it suddenly turned off.

"Oh, no!" Nao exclaimed. "I forgot to charge the batteries on the GPS! We can't map the woods now."

With her quick thinking as always, Leila exclaimed, "Yes we can!" The group eagerly looked toward her with excited interest. She continued, "All we have to do is get out some paper and start tracing our path with that."

Nao continued the line of thinking. "And when we get home, I can put that into the GPS software as a sort of log of where we've been. If we're going to conquer these woods this summer, we need to know where we've been and where we're going." The group nodded in agreement.

Van had a notepad in his pocket, so he pulled it out and handed it to Nao. "You're now the official mapmaker," Van proclaimed in a mock-royalty voice as he touched the edge of his sword upon each of Nao's shoulders.

Nao enjoyed the thought of mapmaking the old-fashioned way. It was a challenge, and Nao was *always* up for a challenge. It should be fun to try and make an accurate, scale map without the aid of technology. The group then had to decide what to do next.

Jeff reminded everyone about the time capsule. "Did everyone bring some stuff to put in the time capsule? Let's get everything out and place it in the container. When we get to a spot that seems just right, we'll be ready to bury it." Everyone else agreed.

Dace brought a computer disk containing one of his favorite video games. He also had a pocketknife that he had won at the state fair a few years back. It was his favorite knife, but that was the point of a time capsule, wasn't it? Wasn't it supposed to hold items of importance or value to their owners? That way, years later, when everyone in the group was really, really old, they could all come back and have a laugh at the ridiculous things they had hidden away in the capsule. The junk hit the capsule with a thud.

Anthony, not realizing they were going to do a time capsule when he was packing for his week-long stay at Dace's house, placed a plastic harmonica into the capsule. Dace laughed because it was a cheapo harmonica that Anthony found that morning in a box of cereal. It and forty-two cents were the only things he had that he could reasonably part with at the time.

Jeff stepped up to the capsule and dropped in a few rare coins and a note to his future self. He thought the coins might be valuable decades later, and the note contained secret information about an undisclosed idea he had that he thought would make him a millionaire in the future.

Leila had the most stuff to put into the capsule. Leila was not a frilly, girly girl by any means, but she still wanted something girly to represent her. She dropped in a pink princess hairbrush, a small copy of her favorite book, two pictures of her pet cat, and a poem she had written about adventure. Everyone begged her to read the poem aloud before dropping it in, so she did. It read as follows:

Into the woods and into my dreams,
I dream of adventure and wonderful things.

What lies ahead for me and my friends,
We hope is a new beginning and not the end.
We'll travel into those exotic woods,
And find hidden treasures and wonderful goods.
I long for adventure so full of promise,
And those carefree times I would never want to miss!

Even though some of the boys were a bit uncomfortable with poetry, everyone was impressed by Leila's writing skills. Dace complimented her on the poem, and Leila tried hard not to blush as she quickly dropped the piece of paper into the time capsule. For a few seconds, time stood still. The thought of adventure and excitement lingered in the minds of the adventurers. For a fleeting moment, there seemed to be magic in the air.

Then Van broke the momentary silence with the squeeze of a whoopee cushion. Always the practical joker, Van dropped in the prank toy and added a fake ice cube with a fly in it. And then, with a twinkle in his eye, he also added what looked like a notepad full of detailed drawings and descriptions. He claimed it was to remind his future self how to pull some of his best pranks just in case his adult self forgot how to be funny. However, no one else in the group could imagine how Van could ever stop being funny.

Finally, the time capsule was complete with Nao's addition of a recording of some of his and Dace's favorite homemade songs. All of their best hits were on there, including the crazy one recorded that night when the pair had gotten a hold of a tuba and a small drum kit from somewhere. Their friends still wondered what happened to those instruments and where they came from. There was a rumor that the now-dented tuba at Nao's church was somehow involved.

With the time capsule filled, Dace sealed it up water-tight and put it in his backpack for later burying. It was at that precise moment when The Woodsmen heard a strange sound that would hasten the discovery of their first great mystery.

"Did you hear that?" asked Jeff, who was nearest to where the sound originated.

"Yeah!" Leila whispered with a hiss. Everyone grew quiet, and their muscles tensed. Leila continued, "As group leader, I'll lead the way toward the sound."

The eerie sound continued its low, moaning whistle. It seemed to come from a point fairly distant from where the group was standing, so they began to hack through the underbrush and push onward toward the sound.

The gang moved tensely and slowly through the woods now. There were a few minor scares as a startled bird took flight here or there. Leila bravely led everyone forward for what seemed like an eternity as they crept their way closer and closer to the sound. After pushing through seemingly endless dense brush, everyone was blinded by the bright, midday sun at an opening near the top of a small waterfall.

At only six or seven feet tall, the waterfall wasn't impressive by any means, but it was still beautiful. Dace and Van both took some pictures, and everyone started goofing around as the tension momentarily evaporated. First, Leila fell into the water when she was trying to climb down a nearby rock face. Her scream startled a flock of birds in the surrounding trees, and they all took flight simultaneously. During the commotion, Nao was trying to remain calm and finish mapping the last few steps of their journey, but he dropped the notepad into the stream. Quickened by the waterfall's force, the stream at the bottom of the falls was much more turbulent than up above. The notepad quickly disappeared somewhere downstream. So much for the map that day!

Leila thought that the boys were staying too dry, so she started pulling them into the water. Dace and Van each hastily protected their cameras from the water as they became drenched in the stuff. Anthony thought it would be funny to make a little flag for their adventure, so he tied a small piece of his now-ripped shirt (the woods weren't forgiving to the adventurer's clothes) to a large stick and stuck it into the soft ground near the waterfall.

"I proclaim this waterfall to be Leila Falls in honor of the first Woodsman to fall in!" yelled Anthony, getting into the spirit of the moment.

Suddenly, Leila yanked Anthony into the water as well, and he got a couple snorts of water before he begged for help from the other guys. Jeff jumped in to save Anthony, but he immediately slipped on the mossy rocks hidden beneath the water's turbulent surface and fell into the now-crowded stream. Everyone splashed about in the shallow water beneath the falls, and they discussed bringing swimsuits and other swimming items next time they ventured into the woods.

After twenty or thirty minutes of playing about in the water, everyone decided it was time to start drying out and continue their journey. While sitting on rocks near the water's edge, the group enjoyed a snack of fruit bars, soy jerky, and trail mix. A couple of the more daring adventurers risked a small drink from the stream, but others warned them it probably wasn't safe. That started a short-lived panic of spitting and rinsing their mouths with water brought from home. All in all it was a good snack.

As their clothes began to dry, the group agreed it was time to move on. They moved away from the waterfall a bit quicker than their previous traveling speed because they stayed near the clearing at the stream's edges. The woods also seemed to be slightly less gnarled and filled with underbrush in that area. Everyone continued to walk and chat about the sorts of things kids always discuss, when suddenly the sound returned!

The Woodsmen had forgotten about the sound since the distraction of the waterfall. They seemed to still be traveling in the general direction of the low moaning, but they still couldn't find the source of the sound.

Remembering the more serious implications of being group leader for the day, Leila told everyone to stop so they could listen more closely. The sound seemed to be coming from a point north and slightly east of where they were. It wasn't a very loud sound, and the group decided that people high up in the neighborhood above the valley probably wouldn't hear it. In fact, at times, the sound seemed to be much quieter and then suddenly much louder. Sometimes it stopped altogether, but it mostly just droned on and on, daring the group to find its source.

They climbed down past another waterfall, trekked up and down some small hills, and continued mostly downward, deeper into the valley between the cliffs. The woods were mostly unexplored and rarely talked about around town. No one (at least adults, anyway) seemed to care much about the woods. The woods probably existed in the valley for thousands of years, but no one gave it much thought.

As the adventurers made their way deeper into the ancient woods, the sky began to fade into a deep blue with a few streaks of orange piercing through some high, wispy clouds. Early evening was upon them.

"Uh, guys, we should probably start to make our way back home. It's starting to get dark," Dace said tentatively. "My mom is expecting us back for dinner, but I don't know if we can even make it back by then."

The urgency of Dace's last statement weighed heavily on the group because they badly wanted to find their way to the source of that eerie sound. However, dinner was an important part of a healthy, growing kid's diet. Especially a spaghetti dinner.

The group warily turned around to go back. Pulling out a rumpled sheet of paper, Nao scribbled some notes about what he thought their relative position was within the woods, and they began to walk back. The going wasn't easy, and the fast-approaching darkness made slips and falls more common. The sense of urgency grew when someone heard a noise nearby that sounded like a coyote. In the daytime, going to the woods was a fun, although intimidating, thing to do, but it could quickly turn into an accident or tragedy waiting to happen when nightfall approached.

As group leader, Leila called for everyone to stay together and keep moving as quickly as possible. They eventually made their way up past the first waterfall, and Nao reckoned they were more than halfway back from their farthest point that day.

Then someone heard the low growling. Before anyone could react, the nearby bushes thrashed about with the sound of something approaching. Without stopping to look, everyone assumed it was a rabid dog or coyote chasing them, and they all took off in a mad dash for the entrance of the woods. When no one was paying attention to the woods' interesting details, travel was much quicker. In only a matter of minutes, they were approaching the woods' entrance. No one noticed that the noise of an approaching menace no longer followed them. They kept running until they burst out of the opening to the woods and continued at top speed until they reached Dace's house a block or so away.

Summer break's first day in the woods ended with a few scratches and bruises, but the adventurers were rewarded with a giant spaghetti dinner, complete with ice cream afterward. Summertime sure was awesome!

Chapter 4
The Great Flood

Even in the summertime friends often had to be apart while they did chores, went on vacations with their families, and rested after days of nonstop playing and adventure. Sometimes even the weather played a part in delaying the plans of the great Woodsmen.

After their first big day in the woods, The Woodsmen dispersed to their respective houses for some rest and relaxation. They planned to get together a few days later to continue their pursuit of the strange noise in the woods. However, on Wednesday clouds rolled into the area. The sky darkened, and the first drops of rain began to fall. Local weathermen said the rain was expected to stick around through the weekend. Everyone knew that the next woods adventure would have to wait until next week at the earliest, and, unfortunately, Anthony had to go home on Saturday.

On Wednesday night, the storms became so fierce that an old, brittle tree was knocked over in Dace's backyard. The next morning when everyone went outside to look at what had happened, they saw strange patterns etched onto the tree by lightning. Luckily, the tree didn't damage anything important other than some broccoli that was growing in Dace's mother's garden. Dace really didn't like broccoli, anyway.

During the rainstorms, Dace, Anthony, and Jeff got together most days to play. Some days they played video games, but when the rain let up, they began what would soon become a summer tradition: sword fights! With the three dull swords that some of the guys had fashioned before their first outing in the woods, Dace, Anthony, and Jeff began their training. They jabbed and dodged, sliced and slid as they tested the limits of the crude metal swords. They imagined they were part of their favorite role-playing video games. Sometimes they even drew up detailed descriptions of their own characters for those games and then acted out the parts during their swordplay.

Mock sword fights lasting late into the evening were often gazed upon in amazement by horrified neighbors who were a little too nosy for their own good. Once, a man from a few houses down rang Dace's parent's doorbell. Dace's older sister, Crystal, answered the door.

"Are your parents home?" asked the man.

"Yeah. Hold on, and I'll get someone," Crystal replied.

Dace's father, Wayne, walked into the kitchen laughing a few minutes later. He turned to Beverly, his wife and Dace's mom, and said, "That was one of our neighbors at the door. He said that Dace and his friends are carelessly playing with *real* swords in the front yard. Well, I walked out there to find that they *did* have metal swords, but the swords were handmade by Dace and his friends. It turns out that they made them at Nao's house, I think, and the swords are pretty dull. I told them to be careful with those things, but I figured they deserve to keep the swords since they did such a good job making them. I also told them to quit playing with the swords in the front yard where the neighbors can see them!"

Beverly looked concerned, but she let it go. Those kids were pretty talented, and she figured they might want the dull swords for their adventures in the woods, anyway.

On Friday night, the begging began. Dace begged his mother to let Anthony stay another week (or longer!), and

Anthony begged his parents to let him stay at Dace's house for another week or so. The boys had so many plans, and they couldn't finish everything by the next day. Eventually, their parents agreed to let Anthony stay longer and that they "would see how it goes" to determine when Anthony would go home. The boys figured this meant Anthony at least got the next week like they wanted. Things would be great if only the rain would stop.

The Woodsmen kept in contact on the phone and online, and they began to call the solid week of rain "The Great Flood." Dace's backyard was mostly a large hill that ended near the stream that eventually ran into the woods. The stream had become so overfilled that it began to slowly flood farther and farther up the hill in the backyard. Dace's wooden clubhouse out back was, luckily, built on stilts so that it stood about eight feet off of the ground. The water lapped at the base of the clubhouse's legs, but the water could never hope to reach the height required to flood it. However, the swing set at the bottom of the hill in the backyard was partially flooded.

All of this water and minor flooding gave Dace and Anthony an Idea. They pushed their way through the piles of boxes and stuff in the garage and set up a small workshop. For a whole day, they sawed, drilled, and hammered on various scraps of wood until they had finished their masterpiece: a raft!

The next morning, the boys finished their breakfast quickly and ran out to the garage to get the raft. It was a lot heavier than they thought it would be. In fact, they could barely drag it to the water's edge in the backyard. They eventually succeeded and pushed the raft into the water. It actually seemed to float! For a moment, that is. As soon as Dace stepped onto the raft, it slowly began to sink. In a moment of panic, Dace jumped off but missed solid ground. He slipped into the muddy flood waters and yelped for help. Anthony dragged a broken tree branch over, and Dace climbed safely out of the water. By that time the raft, half sunk in the water, drifted lazily away downstream and out of reach. So much for their wonderful raft.

The sun came out later that day, and the waters began to recede. The stream was still more than double its normal width and depth, but most of the surrounding area was no longer flooded. With sunny skies ahead, Dace began to plan for The Woodsmen's next official adventure. The water got him to thinking about the most effective ways to travel into the woods. With the stream deeper and faster than normal right then, they could possibly use it as a method of travel. It would be much quicker to make it back to where they had to stop during their last adventure into the woods if they could travel there by water instead of through the dense underbrush.

Quickly, Dace posted a message online to his fellow adventurers. He asked if anyone had a small boat that they could use. Both Nao and Van said they had small inflatable rafts they could use. Each raft held three or four people, so they should be fine. The group also discussed bringing some better methods of offense and defense into the woods in case they met up with a coyote or something even bigger and more ferocious. Jeff said his mom was going to take him to the store that day so he could buy a slingshot, and Dace planned on buying a new machete before their next adventure. The group was going to be better prepared than ever to face whatever hid within the woods.

After some wrangling with parents worried about safety, everyone eventually got permission to go into the woods on the next Wednesday, a little over a week after their first adventure. As before, everyone met at Dace's house in the morning of the agreed-upon day. Everyone was there: Dace, Jeff, Van, Nao, Leila, and Anthony. They looked like a very adventuresome group, ready to conquer anything, and each one had special skills and interests that benefitted the others.

Dace was a bright young boy of nine years. He was of average build, not too tall and not too short, and he was very adventurous. He was often a leader when in groups, but he was happy to let Leila be in charge during their current adventures so that he could concentrate on discovering new things. He loved playing video games, and he played them as often as he could when not playing with friends or doing schoolwork. As for school, Dace, along with his friends Nao, Van, and Leila were homeschooled in their respective homes. Sometimes two or three of the homeschoolers would get together to do some of the lessons to add to the fun and learning.

Jeff, Dace's best friend for the past few years, was a little older than Dace. He was also a little taller than Dace as well. Since Jeff lived just a few blocks away from Dace's house, they got together often. Jeff also loved venturing into the woods, and he (or actually his mother) often bought items that might help them on their adventures.

Van lived in the city about a twenty minute drive away from Dace, and he loved to goof around and play jokes on people, as his friends knew all too well. His fun-loving style helped the adventurers relax a little when things got too serious.

Nao lived about a mile away from Dace's house and was in many ways also Dace's best friend. Nao was intelligent, shrewd, and, as Leila put it, "kind of geeky." He was a loyal friend and determined adventurer who always seemed to figure out a way to get the group out of trouble when the situation seemed impossible.

Leila had been friends with Dace for a couple years after meeting him at a large homeschool get-together. They often did schoolwork together when one of their mothers wanted a day off from teaching school. Leila was a fun girl to be around, and she considered herself to be just one of the boys to some extent. She was always ready to go on an adventure with the guys.

Anthony, Dace's cousin from another city a couple hours drive away, was often quiet and reserved. However, adventure seemed to bring out his more outgoing side, and he was known to be the wild one at times when adventure was on the line. He would watch the backs of the group and make sure no harm came to them.

As the six adventurers stood there waiting for Dace's mom to take some pictures, they certainly did look like a good match for each other. They appeared as if they could take on anything, even as young as they were, with an average age of only ten years old!

When Dace's mom was done with the pictures, Nao and Van started blowing up their rafts. The rafts were small, but it still took what seemed like forever to fill them completely with air. As soon as the rafts were filled, the adventurers immediately tossed the bouncy, rubbery blobs into the water and loaded them up with gear and people. They were soon floating down the stream toward the entrance of the woods and toward a second adventure that could change their lives forever. The Great Flood of that summer turned out to be a truly great thing after all.

Chapter 5
Mystery and Discovery

Floating and sometimes paddling down the stream proved to be a much quicker form of transportation than walking. The group quickly approached the entrance of the woods. After stopping momentarily to take a few pictures and start the GPS device's tracking feature for their map, they went in through the stream entrance into the woods.

As they floated along, everyone was able to focus more on what was around them than the first time. Instead of chopping away at underbrush and getting poked with thorns, they could listen to the birds chirping and watch the various types of plants go by. They saw blue jays and even a scissor-tailed flycatcher fly past. They noticed gnawing at the base of a few trees and wondered if there were any beavers living in the area. Many tadpoles were seen darting through the water, waiting for the day when their new legs would send them leaping upon land. The group continued to float at a comfortable pace down the stream as they watched the wonders of nature drift by.

"Look! There's where Nao was attacked by a giant rabbit!" joked Van. "I bet Slasher is still secretly watching us, making sure we don't get into too much trouble."

Later, Leila remarked, "Hey, I hear some splashing up ahead. I think we're getting close to the first waterfall already."

After a few more minutes, the group climbed out of the rafts and pulled their backpacks onto their backs. As they approached the edge at the top of the waterfall, they tossed the air-filled rafts softly down onto the ground below. Next, they each climbed down to the bottom and got back into the rafts, once again floating upon the stream. The adventure continued in this somewhat laid-back fashion until they heard the strange noise again for the first time that day. Then everyone remembered that this adventure was far from a simple trip down a stream. It was potentially filled with danger at every turn, and mysteries were waiting to be solved.

As they approached the point that Nao believed was the farthest point they had reached on their last journey, they stopped. Everyone got out of the rafts and pulled them to shore. The total time traveled on the stream was less than an hour! Previously, it had taken them most of the day to reach this point within the woods. While traveling on the rafts was a fast way to get into the woods, the group wanted to explore on land from here on so that they wouldn't miss any important details.

Everyone got out of the rafts and readied themselves for travel by foot. A few of them got out swords, Jeff got out his new slingshot, and Dace wielded his new machete. The rafts had to be deflated and packed away before they could start walking, and this took longer than they had planned.

While the guys were working on the rafts, Leila decided to scout ahead. She pushed her way through about fifty feet of brush and approached one side of the valley. As she gazed up at the sheer rock face ahead, she noticed something to the left side on the rocks. It looked like a crack in the rocks. Leila strolled over to investigate the crack and found that it was just wide enough for a person to fit through, and it went all the way up to the top of the cliff. She also noticed that the eerie sound was much louder near the crack. Deciding that it would be best not to go in alone, she turned to go back toward the guys. Suddenly, from out of the crack, something gripped Leila on the back of her neck! She screamed in horror.

The guys had just finished packing the first raft and were deflating the second one when they heard the scream. Dace, Anthony, and Jeff left Nao and Van to finish with the raft while they went to investigate the scream. Since they assumed it must be Leila, they started to run in her direction. The underbrush clawed at them and tore into their clothes, but they pressed forward as fast as they could.

Moments later, the guys reached the point from which they thought the scream came, but there was no one there. They looked around and noticed the big crack in the rock face. They called out for Leila, but she didn't answer. Worried that something terrible had happened, the guys started back toward Nao and Van. Nao and Van had just finished packing the second raft when the other guys approached.

"Leila's missing, and we think she is the one who just screamed!" blurted Dace in a panic.

Nao, always the level-headed one, said, "We should begin to search for her immediately in a systematic way. Let's form two groups and spread out to look for her. I have the GPS so I can track the progress of my group, and we can keep in contact with these walkie-talkies."

"What! I didn't know we had walkie-talkies with us! Leila could have taken one and stayed in contact with us while she was exploring," Dace said in an exasperated voice.

"I forgot I brought them because I had so much stuff packed. And besides, I didn't think we'd lose somebody right after we got out of the boats," Nao replied.

Jeff broke in, "Guys, let's not waste time, here. Leila could be anywhere, and we know she screamed, so she's probably in trouble. What if she fell off of something or got bitten by a snake?"

Bringing up snakes suddenly got everyone worried. Quickly, they finished packing their gear, divided into two groups, and started looking for Leila. Nao was the head of Group Alpha with Van. He figured that with the GPS helping them keep track, they would only need two people. Dace was the head of Group Beta with Anthony and Jeff.

Group Beta went back toward the crack in the rocks since they had been there before and knew the way. Group Alpha went farther downstream to see if Leila had gotten lost and might be able to at least find the stream. They all assumed she hadn't crossed the stream since it was fairly deep just then, but she still could have done so pretty easily.

As Dace's group investigated around the crack in the rocks, they noticed that the eerie sound was louder there. Dace decided to go in and investigate more closely since Leila may have thought it would be safe inside the rocky protection.

Dace let Nao know what they were doing. "We're going inside a crack in the rock face to the right of where we got out of the rafts. That weird sound is louder here, also, so we're going to see if we can find anything out about that while we're in here."

"We'll keep looking around out here. I'm kind of getting a weird feeling about this, though. Maybe we should stop calling out her name in case it was a kidnapper who got her. We don't want them to know we're about to find them," replied Nao over the walkie-talkie.

"Okay. I'll get back to you over the walkie-talkie in a few minutes. If anything happens where we can't talk, meet up with us back where we got off the rafts near the stream," Dace said.

"All right. Nao out."

Dace's Group Beta entered the crack in the rocks and quietly crept along so as not to make any noise. Still, leaves crunched underfoot and small rocks scattered about as they went along. The path within the crack got a little wider after a while and wound around to the left. Sunlight seeped down from far above for the first few minutes of the journey, but eventually heavy brush and trees at the top of the cliffs filtered out most of the light. The team got out their flashlights and continued farther into the crevice.

Just when the path had started to narrow and Dace didn't think they were going to find Leila in there, the guys heard a noise up ahead. The noise was almost drowned out by the eerie sound that had gotten louder the deeper they had gone into the passageway, but they heard the quiet shuffling anyway. The noise floated on the cool air that gently drifted through the passageway. It sounded like someone was walking toward them! Quickly but quietly, the guys pulled out their weapons and prepared for the worst. Maybe a wolf was preparing to attack them from out of the shadows. Maybe a den of poisonous snakes was slithering its way toward the boys and would, at any moment, devour them in a writhing mess of fangs and scales.

Then Leila's face appeared up ahead. She shouted in surprise when she saw the guys armed with their weapons. "What are you doing? How did you find me here? And why do you have those weapons drawn?" she asked, astonished.

"Are you okay?" Dace quickly asked with concern. "We thought you were dead or something! We heard you scream."

"Oh, that," Leila replied with a smirk. "A big spider dropped down onto my neck from the rocks above. I thought it bit me for a minute until I realized I had clawed my own neck while frantically trying to get the spider off of me."

"Well, I'm glad you're fine, but why didn't you come

back and let us know what happened? Nao and Van are still out there looking for you. Actually, I need to call him on the walkie-talkie real quick," Dace said. He called Nao and let him know that they had found Leila and that everyone was fine. Nao said that he and Van would meet the others in the passageway.

"Now, why didn't you come back and tell us what was going on? You're the leader, after all. You're supposed to act responsibly," Dace demanded.

Leila replied, "I was about to go back, but that strange noise was louder in here, and I just wanted to see if I could find more out about it real quick before I went back. I didn't even think you guys heard me scream. It wasn't very loud, was it?"

The guys laughed, and Jeff said, "It was so loud, I bet every bird in the woods took flight in one second! It was amazing!" They all laughed.

Then Dace asked Leila, "Did you find anything in here, or are we just wasting our time looking for that sound?"

Leila's face suddenly got very serious-looking, and she replied in a hushed, almost reverent voice, "I think I found something."

Just then, the group heard Nao and Van calling from the entrance of the passageway, and Anthony, at the back of the group in the passageway, yelled for them to come in and meet up with everyone else. When the whole Woodsmen gang was reunited, Leila told them to follow her deeper into the passageway.

The group walked forward for a while, and the eerie noise grew louder. At one point, each person carefully squeezed through a very small opening in the rock that they thought an adult could never get through. It abruptly got very dark within the passageway as the sky and trees overhead were obscured by solid rock. At that point, the group stopped.

"This is as far as I got before I decided to turn around and go back to get you guys," Leila said as she turned to face the group. "Do you know what this is?" she asked in a way that betrayed she already probably knew the answer.

Nao quickly replied, "It appears to be the entrance to a cave!" Everyone started getting more and more excited as Nao continued, "Judging by where we found this entrance and by how difficult it is to get to this point, we could have found a new cave that has never been explored before!"

"Then no one knows about this place!" exclaimed Anthony. He rarely got worked up about things unless they were really important. Besides, he was on an important adventure making discoveries at that very moment. He knew they had found something special.

The eerie noise got louder for a moment, and a chilled wind rushed past the group and out through the passageway. Leila got chill bumps on her arms, but the bumps were there more from excitement than from the cool air. Jeff noticed Leila's chill bumps as well as his own, and he suddenly wanted to get out of there for no apparent reason. It was starting to feel very cramped and spooky in that place.

"Uh, guys, maybe we should get back out to the woods. It might be getting late, and I'm starting to get a little hungry. Oh yeah, and I think I left something back near the stream," Jeff babbled without really convincing anyone of what he was saying, including himself. He started to get slightly embarrassed when he realized no one else seemed to want to turn back.

Then Nao spoke up, somewhat in Jeff's defense, "Actually, while I do think we should explore ahead for a while, we are going to have to go back a little earlier tonight because we not only have to make our way back out of the cave and passageway, but we are also going to have to get out of the woods on foot or re-inflate the rafts and paddle against the current. Either way, it's going to take a lot longer to get out of the woods than it took to get in, and I don't want to get caught out here in the dark again."

Everyone agreed that they would keep the cave exploring short and give themselves plenty of time to exit the woods that evening. Even with flashlights, the woods were an intimidating maze of vegetation, rocks, and traps when a person couldn't see ahead very far. However, the group still wanted to explore the cave right then because they didn't yet know what secrets they might uncover. Anything could be waiting in there, unseen by humans since the beginning of time. And it is often the great unknown that disrupts the best plans and corrupts the best intentions. The cave begged—demanded—that The Woodsmen enter into its hidden depths. Turning back was impossible.

Chapter 6
Into the Tunnel

"Light! I need more light!" screeched Van as he attempted to peer further into the entrance to the cave.

Everyone quickly shone their flashlights into the darkness ahead. Very little could be seen with their puny flashlights. About fifteen or twenty feet ahead the light faded away into nothingness. The group figured they weren't going to be able to do as much exploring as they could with better flashlights (they hadn't brought bigger lights since they didn't expect to be out of the sunlight except for a short period on the way back home that evening), but the small, dim lights were all they currently had. They would have to make do with those as best as they could.

In his best ghostly-sounding voice, Van breathed, "So, who wants to enter into the lair of darkness?" At that moment, the eerie sound blew out through the cave entrance and was once more accompanied by a cool breeze. Van shuddered.

"Ah-hah!" Nao unexpectedly blurted. "I know the reason for the eerie sound!" Everyone looked toward Nao in anticipation of the answer to their first big mystery. "There are probably some openings in the cave that allow wind from up above to blast down into the cave at times. The cave's properties must combine with the wind to make that strange moaning sound."

Nao's explanation made sense, and everyone accepted his theory as a pretty reasonable explanation for the eerie sound. After revealing that the eerie sound was probably nothing more than wind, the group felt a little more at ease. They decided to enter the cave.

As The Woodsmen pressed on, they began to realize that this cave was like a natural tunnel carved out of solid rock over the centuries (or more!). Some of them thought it could have been made by an underground river, and others thought it might have been made by more interesting means, like by an ancient volcano or a giant earthquake. Whatever the case might have been, they started referring to it as "the tunnel" without even realizing it. And the tunnel was amazing.

Although it was shaped more like a tunnel than the large rooms and pockets within many caves, the tunnel still had many interesting features. Formations such as stalactites were found in many places, clinging to the rocky ceiling and dripping water down on passersby. Stalagmites were also present, standing tall and proud upon the ground, daring the adventurers to crawl over or squeeze past the mighty stone statues.

The tunnel was damp everywhere, and water dripped down on the cave adventurers' heads. The flashlight beams glimmered off of shiny surfaces and revealed intricate details forever carved into the solid stone. A few strange bugs crawled here or there about the rock, and the group noticed some small fish in one of the water pools.

The group had only cautiously traversed what seemed like a short distance within the dark tunnel when it suddenly split into three different directions. The left direction seemed to be similar to what they had just walked through: fairly large and open with a relatively level walkway. The middle passage was marked by a small opening that led into a cramped tube that would require crawling to get through. The opening on the right was seven or eight feet across and appeared normal enough until Anthony casually shone his flashlight into it and discovered that the passageway dropped straight down for at least the first twenty feet. Past that, he couldn't see clearly because his flashlight was too weak. They would definitely need ropes to explore that one.

"Since we don't have a lot of time, I think we should go with what looks like the easiest path," Leila said convincingly as group leader.

No one had any reasonable objection to Leila's idea other than that a few of them thought it would be fun to try and squeeze into the small middle passageway. However, it looked very tight, and no one was sure if they could even fit. Clearer heads prevailed, and the group went with the passageway on the left.

The left passageway in the tunnel seemed to be about the same as the tunnel's entrance passageway at first, but Dace noticed a difference as he was examining one of the walls to the side. "Hey, everybody, come look at this!" he called out as he peered at something on the wall.

It turned out that Dace wasn't just peering *at* something, but *into* something. It was a small room! The naturally-made room was almost like a small bedroom off of a main hallway. It had a few chunky parts in the rock where small ledges jutted out like shelves on the wall. There was even a smooth-topped boulder that had fallen over in the corner. It looked a lot like a bed. And off to one side of the room, there was a small opening looking out into the passageway like a little window.

"This is *awesome*!" exclaimed Van. "I could certainly get used to a bedroom like this where the walls don't have to be repainted after a practical joke gets out of hand. And my parents can't tell me to take out the trash because I'm *underground*!"

Everyone laughed at Van's antics as he continued to joke about the benefits of living in a cave. At one point, somebody started jumping around and acting like a caveman, and then they all got into the act.

Leila was the cavewoman mother who came in to tell her children it was time for dinner. "I have some nice woolly mammoth stew for you all to eat!" she said proudly to her "children."

Jeff grunted in his best caveman voice, "I will go get some sticks for the fire tonight, mother. It's been very cold since this ice age rolled through the village." And on they went, playing like cave people and having fun in their new-found home underground.

After some time had passed, Dace began to wonder what time it was. He had forgotten to wear his watch since it wasn't that important outside where one can see when it is getting dark, so he asked Nao, who always had the latest time-telling gadget ("It also plays video games and has a calculator," Nao would often brag to his watch admirers).

"We still have about two hours before dark," Nao answered Dace's time question. "We should probably leave the tunnel in no more than an hour." Everyone reluctantly agreed. They were having a lot of fun in their secret cave.

After a while, the group left the little bedroom and explored farther into the passageway. They found a few more room-like openings off to the sides of the tunnel, and then they came to a fairly large body of water that was as wide as the passageway and continued forward at least as far as their wimpy flashlights could see. They decided to stop and eat, then turn back and head home for the day.

Dace opened the wrapper to a delicious granola bar with chocolate chips and took a big bite. He hadn't noticed how hungry he'd become during all of the excitement of losing Leila, finding the passageway to the cave entrance, and finally beginning to explore within the tunnel. In fact, no one in the group had eaten since breakfast, and it was already nearing dinner time. Everyone began to eat hungrily. It got very quiet on the shore of the cave pool, except for the munching sounds of the hungry adventurers.

Suddenly, everyone jumped when a noise startled them from above. Bats! Dozens of bats were flying past overhead! It wasn't like the swarms Dace had heard about that came out of large caves in some parts of the world, but it was still a big group of bats flying by. Dace figured that the bats must be flying out to begin their evening mealtime of millions of bugs. Gross. And yet, still kind of cool, he thought.

The group admired the bats flying past, and Anthony, unfortunately, was hit by some bat guano (simply bat poop to the common observer) from a bat that had momentarily stopped for a rest on the ceiling above. This time everyone laughed except for Anthony. However, Leila, compassionate as always, gave him an extra napkin to clean it off.

"Just don't accidently use that to wipe the chocolate chips and granola off of your mouth afterward," Leila joked with Anthony. He actually cracked a smile after that.

Anthony, along with everyone else, was beginning to realize that Leila was really a good leader for their group. She wasn't afraid to lead them into the unknown and stay ahead of the pack even when danger might be right around the corner. She was fearless in some ways but also still compassionate. She helped lend a softer edge to their adventures when the guys might have been at a loss to decide how to do something the best way, and she was always ready to help out regardless of the challenge involved. Anthony was thinking that Leila might make a good long-term leader beyond just their immediate adventure into the woods.

After the bats had all flown by and the group was done eating, they decided to check out the cave pool in more detail before leaving for the day. Nao couldn't get a reading on his GPS because they were down in the cave, but he was trying to determine how far in they had come to reach the pool. Jeff and Van were sticking their hands in the water and remarking that it felt very cool and refreshing. Dace tried to determine how deep the water was by shining his flashlight straight down. The super-clear, clean water was easy to see through, and Dace thought the pool looked about ten feet deep. Leila was trying to see how far across the pool was by reflecting her light off of the water's surface, but the flashlight was still too weak to yield any helpful results.

Once about thirty more minutes had passed and the group had examined the water without getting in or trying to swim, they decided it was time to head back home. Nao started drawing a map of the left passageway of the tunnel as the gang made their way back to the main passageway. He then made notes about the characteristics that he could see of the other passageway entrances, and he continued drawing his map on the way out of the main tunnel.

Dace had a wonderful idea as the group exited the tunnel. He suggested that they bury their time capsule—which they hadn't had time to bury before—right there in the ground near the entrance to the tunnel. It was the perfect place. No one could easily get to the area, animals didn't appear to dig around back in there, and everyone could easily remember where they buried the capsule by placing it there. The Woodsmen agreed, and a couple of the guys started digging with little shovels they had brought specifically for burying the capsule. They dug deep enough so that nothing would accidently dig it up, and then they had a small ceremony to commemorate the event.

"I declare that this day be called 'Time Capsule Day' in honor of our special capsule being buried here," Leila proclaimed as the official leader of the group.

"I'm going to record the location on the GPS so we'll know exactly where both the cave entrance and the time capsule are," Nao noted as he tapped away on the device.

Dace mentioned, "Maybe we ought to make a sign for the entrance to the tunnel and to mark this spot. Of course, we won't put that there's a time capsule buried here!" And with that remark, the time capsule ceremony was complete.

After burying the time capsule, the group squeezed through the little opening in the rock that led them back out to daylight, shimmied through the thin passageway between the cliffs, and finally made their way back to the point at the stream where they had exited the rafts earlier in the day. At that point, it was definitely evening time, and the group had to make a decision. Should they walk back through the woods, hacking their way through the under-brush, or should they paddle against the current in the stream? Ultimately, they decided to walk back, since blowing up the rafts was a hard chore and took a pretty long time if done without a powered air pump.

As they hacked their way back toward the entrance to the woods, the group discussed their secret findings.

"First of all, I think we shouldn't tell anyone about the tunnel, at least until we know more about it," Jeff said.

"Yeah, but what if next time we're in the tunnel, somebody tries to contact us, but they can't find us. I mean, at least our parents know we're in the woods, but there's no way they could find us in that cave. No one knows about it, and an adult would have a hard time squeezing through that small hole in the rock before you get to the tunnel's entrance. If we died in there, they might never find us," Dace commented as he hacked away at overgrown, thorny bushes and weeds.

"I think it might be a good idea not to tell anyone even though it might not be as safe. In fact, we can't tell anyone exactly *because* it is dangerous. That'd be the last time we go into the woods or the tunnel for sure!" Van lamented.

Everyone was a little uneasy about keeping the tunnel a secret, but they knew what Van said was true. If they were really the only ones who knew about that cave, it would have to stay that way if they ever hoped to explore it further. So it was decided. The group made a pact to not tell anyone—*not anyone*—about the tunnel until they all agreed to do otherwise. That agreement would probably be a long time away until they had explored the tunnel fully. Little did they know, the tunnel held many more secrets for them to uncover, and it would be a long time before they could explore it in enough depth to uncover all of those secrets.

The adventurers finally made their way out of the woods as the sun was setting. The triumphant Woodsmen returned to Dace's house expecting a quick dinner before they had to go home, but they were all in for another surprise that day.

"Hi, Dace," Crystal said when the group came in through the front door. "We're going out for pizza and bowling tonight! I've been setting up a slumber party tonight with my friends, and mom said we can all go out first!"

Surprisingly, The Woodsmen suddenly found themselves very tired and not as excited about bowling as they normally would be, but they were all *very* excited about going out for pizza. Dace always thought pizza was the best summer food, anyway, and it was the perfect end to another long day of adventure in the woods.

Chapter 7
Hard Work and Fun Days

The next week, Anthony had to leave for home. Dace and Anthony pleaded for days and told their parents all of the reasons why it was critical that Anthony stay another few weeks, but it was of no use. Anthony forgot that he had a summer camp to go to later that week, and his mother said she had some work for him to do, anyway.

Dace promised Anthony that he'd be kept up-to-date on the happenings of The Woodsmen, and the boys even secured a promise from their parents that Anthony would be able to stay again later that summer. As Anthony's parents arrived to pick him up from Dace's house, Dace reminded Anthony about the secret.

"Remember. No one can ever know. Well, at least not for now," Dace whispered into Anthony's ear as they walked together out the front door.

"I promise," Anthony replied. And with that, The Woodsmen, at least for a while, became a group of only five.

Dace, disappointed and a bit depressed that day, went back inside to think. To help him think, he started playing video games. Games always had a way of relaxing him while at the same time sharpening his problem-solving skills. Sometimes when he was working on a big, in-game mystery, he would suddenly realize the solution to a real-life problem. Games were just like that for Dace.

The first problem that Dace was working on was

how to cross the cave pool in the left passageway. The group could never hope to explore further without some easy method of crossing the water. Sure, they could swim across easily enough (assuming the water didn't go on for a lengthy distance), but they'd be wet and either have to change clothes or simply live with being wet the rest of the day while in the cave. Another issue with swimming was that they didn't know what was in that water. What if some cave creature silently glided up from the hidden depths and swallowed one of them whole? What if the liquid actually turned out to be some kind of weird cave acid and burned their skin? The truth was that they were simply too afraid to swim across, and it was inconvenient, anyway.

Then Dace thought about using the rafts to cross the water. They should work perfectly to get across a few times, but they would also be inconvenient for long-term use. To even get the rafts inside the cave would require deflating them and passing them through the small opening that lead to the entrance. Next, they would have to re-inflate the rafts inside the cave, which was time-consuming. Finally, if they didn't want to leave one or both of the rafts in the cave permanently, they'd have to deflate them and take them back out. They would have to do all of that *every time* they wanted to use the rafts in the cave. The rafts might work for some exploration, but the group would need a more-permanent solution for long-term use.

As Dace sat there playing an adventure video game, he suddenly realized what the hero of the game used to cross small streams and pools of water: a bridge! Now of course within the game world, the hero somehow magically carried around this heavy bridge that could span any length of water that the hero was supposed to cross. In the real world, the gang would need to build some sort of collapsible bridge that could be taken apart and reassembled in the tunnel when the time came. That was going to take some hard work, some free (and not-so-free) wood from a variety of sources, and days of construction and planning. Dace was beginning to think he needed to hire some help! Or maybe the group just needed an extra pair of hands to get the work done in a timely fashion.

Later that evening, Dace was chatting with Nao and Jeff online about the bridge idea. Nao thought it was a great idea, but he said they should take some measurements in the cave to make sure they were building the right size of bridge. Jeff said he could probably convince his younger brother, Kevin (about three years younger than Jeff—two years younger than Dace), to help them if they promised that Jeff could be part of the adventure. Also, Kevin might come in handy when the larger guys couldn't squeeze through a small opening within the tunnel. Nao mentioned that Kevin would be helpful in mapping and exploring the cave due to his size. They all agreed to recruit Kevin as a part-time member of The Woodsmen.

Of course, before recruiting a new member for a small group, the other members of the group should be asked about it first. Van and Leila both thought it was a good idea to recruit Kevin, at least as a part-time member, but Leila was concerned that Kevin might tell others about their discovery. That was a very important point. Kevin could destroy their plans just by saying the wrong thing to the wrong person. Jeff said that he'd handle that part of the deal, and Kevin would definitely not say anything about the tunnel to anyone. Everyone else trusted that Jeff could handle Kevin, so they all agreed to admit a new member into The Woodsmen.

A few days later, Dace and Nao went back to the tunnel to take some measurements. This adventure wasn't about exploring or discovery, so the boys walked quickly and treated the measuring more like a business than like an adventure. Nao measured the width of various things: the small opening that lead to the tunnel entrance, the entrance itself, and the average width of the left passageway within the tunnel. As Nao called out measurements, Dace wrote them down. They brought along large, powerful flashlights this time so that they could hopefully see across the cave pool. They estimated that the pool was only a little over twenty feet in length, just barely out of range for their flashlights when they were last in the tunnel. They also noticed that the passageway continued on much farther into the distance past the pool of water.

Dace and Nao then went to investigate the entrance to the middle passageway. It was a small hole just barely smaller than either of the boys could fit through. Kevin would probably fit just perfectly. When they shined their lights through the opening, they could only see a solid rock wall about ten feet ahead, and then the tight, tube-like passageway seemed to curve off to the right.

The boys then examined the entrance to the right passageway off of the main tunnel. The entrance was almost as large as the main tunnel itself, but it immediately dropped down a sheer rock wall about twenty-five or thirty feet. After that, it looked like the passageway leveled off considerably and was fairly smooth. With some strong rope, they could rappel down that wall and, eventually, build a ladder going up and down the entire distance. This cave was going to be a lot of work!

After the boys' quick day of measuring things in the tunnel, they started writing up a plan on what to build and what to bring for their next big exploration adventure. Dace also remembered that they were going to make a sign for the tunnel's entrance. And so they planned a series of hard-work construction days for The Woodsmen to complete. However, even though they were going to be working hard, that didn't mean they couldn't have any fun! The boys also planned a water balloon and shaving cream fight for day one, a basketball tournament on the next day, and finally a cookout and huge bonfire on the third day. It was going to be a busy week.

The next day everyone went over to Nao's house because he had the best workshop where they could build things. Everyone brought what wood and other building-related items they could find or beg from their parents. Dace had some money saved up from doing chores and running his neighborhood candy stand, so he bought some of the main wood beams they would need for bridge construction. The group had also decided to build some chairs, benches, and a table for inside the tunnel. There was some discussion about building stuff for the small rooms they had found in the left passageway, but no one could agree upon whose room was whose without going back to the tunnel and looking around some more. The bedroom furniture would have to wait.

"Let's build the bridge in multiple, small sections that can be fit together and permanently bolted or screwed together down in the cave. A bridge this long isn't going to be easy to build or move, but it's going to be awesome once we finish it!" Nao said as he starting measuring and marking some wood beams.

The other members of the group started cutting, drilling, and bolting parts together. Nao had found some plans on the Internet that showed how to build a simple, flat bridge to span short distances like the one in the tunnel. He and Van (who had spent the night at Nao's house the night before), made some changes to the plans so the bridge would fit their needs.

The work was going along smoothly, and lunchtime came quickly. Nao's mom, Nayoko, was an excellent cook. She made the most wonderful blueberry muffins, cherry cake, and apple pie! But desserts weren't the only things she could make. Her pizza sticks were delicious! Dace always asked her for the secret recipe to the pizza sauce, but Nayoko never revealed that it was simply a can of name-brand pizza sauce from the store. She always just said, "Maybe I'll give your mom the recipe someday."

That day, lunch didn't consist of blueberry muffins or pizza sticks. It was a new recipe that Nayoko had been wanting to try out on the kids. It was kind of like a chicken cordon bleu—a chicken-and-cheese-filled bread wrap. And it was awesome. Being the excellent chef that she was, Nayoko didn't simply fill the wraps with chicken and cheese. She also added steamed vegetables and some spices that made it burst with flavor in the kids' mouths. Dace thought that the group had been eating *very* well that summer.

After the excellent lunch, the group returned to their construction process. The various parts of the bridge were nearly complete when Dace suddenly remembered that they were going to make a sign for the tunnel entrance. Van immediately volunteered for the job because he had some ideas about how the sign should look. Everyone else finished the bridge while Van artfully cut out a shape for the sign and began painting it.

When the sign was done, Van revealed it to the others. Everyone was impressed by Van's art skills, and they just had to laugh at the funny shape he had made. The sign was shaped like a big mouth, and the mouth was saying, "Beware of The Woodsmen." There was also, for some strange reason, a hand holding a menacing-looking fish. That was part of Van's strange sense of humor. The group liked the sign and thought it was just weird enough that it fit perfectly with their strange cave, so full of mystery and fun.

After the first day of work, the group had finished the bridge and was ready for the water balloon and shaving cream fight at Dace's house. Everyone rode their bikes over to Dace's and started filling balloons. Crystal and a few of her friends were also going to be in on the fun that evening. Once everything was ready, the games began.

Things started simply enough when Dace shot Crystal with some shaving cream. Then everyone went crazy as water-filled balloons began to fly. For a few minutes, Nao and Van ganged up against the other kids, but the alliance didn't last long once Van took the opportunity to dump a huge bucket of water on Nao's head when his back was turned. Jeff somehow managed to become completely covered with shaving cream, and Kevin brought out his secret weapon: the Giant Soaker! As Kevin started blasting away with his new water gun, Dace's dad, Wayne Hatch, got home from work. When Mr. Hatch—wearing a new suit for a big legal case he was arguing that day—stepped out of the car, he was instantly soaked from blasting water guns and flying water balloons. Needless to say, Mr. Hatch wasn't smiling at that point. However, he didn't say anything. He just walked inside the house.

Since Dace's dad didn't stop the water fight, the kids continued to play. A few minutes later they had forgotten about the incident with Mr. Hatch, and the fight was nearly over. Just then, Mr. Hatch came out of nowhere with a water hose, which was firing a million gallons a minute (or so it seemed). He laughed like a maniac while he soaked everyone to the bone with the hose. The kids noticed that he was now wearing some swim trunks instead of a business suit. That meant it was time to get him back.

All at once, the kids started throwing the last water balloons at Dace's dad, and a couple of the kids shot the last shaving cream from their bottles. Mr. Hatch was outmatched. Even a water hose couldn't hold back the fury of nine kids all hitting him with bombs and shaving cream. Game over.

After everyone had a good laugh and did a bunch of cleaning up, the day was over. A few of the guys stayed the night at Dace's house, and everyone agreed to meet again at Nao's the next day to start building their furniture.

That evening before bedtime, Dace's dad asked him what the kids had been working on so hard. Dace told him it was a bridge for their adventures. His dad was impressed that the kids were putting so much time and hard work into something that he decided to help pay for some of the adventure supplies the group said they needed. Things were really looking up for the tunnel crew. Soon The Woodsmen were going to have an excellent bridge, some custom furniture, and some spelunking gear to help explore the cave. Of course, that type of gear could be used for exploring the woods as well.

The next day, everyone met again at Nao's house and began constructing simple tables and chairs. The furniture couldn't be completely put together there since it had to fit into the tunnel opening. They would have to finish the last parts of construction down within the cave. After the furniture-building day, a basketball tournament was held behind Nao's house. Kevin was pretty good at basketball, even being shorter than the other kids, and he was voted the MVP of the game. Everyone had a lot of fun, but they were exhausted by the end of the day.

On the final day of construction, the kids were getting eager to get back to the woods and into the tunnel. They could hardly wait to finish the final pieces and pack everything up for the journey to the tunnel. After stacking up all of the almost-finished pieces for transportation to and through the woods, the group realized that they would have to make multiple trips. The rafts could only hold a few pieces of furniture or a few pieces of the bridge at a time. They figured it would take three trips to get all of the pieces to the entrance of the tunnel.

Finally, everything was stacked up and ready to transport into the woods. First, they would have to load the pieces into a minivan and have them driven over to Dace's house. The actual trips wouldn't take place until the next week when Leila, Jeff, and Kevin were back in town. Leila was visiting her grandparents in a different town for a few days, and Jeff and Kevin were going on a vacation with their parents for about a week.

The last thing The Woodsmen did together before splitting up for a week was to build a huge bonfire in Leila's backyard (she lived near the edge of town and had a big backyard) and roast marshmallows to add to chocolate and graham crackers. Leila's parents helped the kids cook some other good foods out over the fire as well, and everyone told campfire stories about adventure and danger. The Woodsmen took those stories to heart and realized that danger and adventure went hand-in-hand.

The chocolate was great, and the adventurers were looking forward to the next week. However, everybody really needed a long rest before their next big adventure in the woods. With solemn goodbyes, The Woodsmen went their separate ways. That night, they each dreamed of the glorious adventures that still awaited them deep within the neighborhood woods.

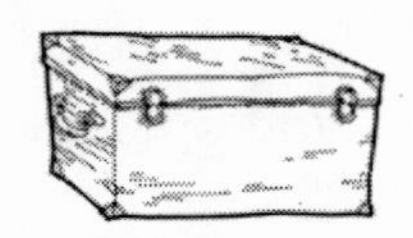

Chapter 8
Moving In

Midsummer was approaching fast, and the summer heat was scorching outside. Plants of every type were in full bloom and overgrowing in every direction. Out in the woods, the plants seemed to be growing thicker than ever before. Gnarled vines hugged some of the trees. Underbrush snaked its way across the ground while thorns lay in wait to poke passersby. Bugs swarmed in some areas, and mosquitoes were biting in full force. It was the dog days of summer. It was the time when even kids who loved to play outside were staying in the shade and yearning for lemonade and a fan.

The six kids who now comprised the group known as The Woodsmen—Dace, Jeff, Kevin, Leila, Nao, and Van (Anthony was temporarily away)—definitely loved the outdoors. Each one loved adventure and wanted to explore the woods and the tunnel more fully. However, even they were more interested in going underground into the cool air of the cave than exploring outside in the woods. They had planned a multiple-day adventure for their third (and possibly final for that year) big trip into the woods, and they knew that the first day of moving stuff was going to be the hardest with the sun beating down mercilessly.

It was going to be a long day, but The Woodsmen knew they'd still have fun. As soon as they could get all of their custom-built things into the tunnel, they could begin to move in for real. Well, at least they dreamed of moving in. They knew they couldn't actually live in the cave in the woods, but they sure could spend as much time there as possible.

Over the past week while most of the group was relaxing or taking trips, Dace worked on a special project with his dad. They built a wooden box that could be taken apart easily for transportation and put back together for storage of equipment. Dace wanted a box like this for the tunnel so that the group could store some items there permanently instead of transporting them back and forth. He even added a metal loop on the box for a padlock in case strangers did somehow discover the gang's secret hideout. Even though many people knew about The Woodsmen's adventures, no one knew about the tunnel itself except for The Woodsmen.

On a sunny Wednesday morning, everyone met to begin their so-called moving day. The first order of business was to figure out how to transport the many items. Some items were long but still fairly thin so that they could fit through the tight openings leading to the tunnel. Other items were small but heavy. Because there had been no rain for a while and the temperatures were high, the stream running into the woods was much lower than during their last adventure. The rafts could not be used to travel on the stream like the group first thought they could be, so everything would have to be carried by hand. Travel would be slow.

They decided to have Kevin chop down the underbrush and clear a path through the woods since he was the smallest and could have carried the least. Everyone else picked up as much stuff as they could carry and began the trip into the woods. As they slowly pushed their way through the plants, the group needed to stop and take frequent breaks. This was starting to feel like real work! Even though the going was tough, everyone knew it would be worth it in the end.

The Woodsmen made four trips into the woods that

day and stacked up everything they carried near the crack in the rock face that marked the passage leading to the tunnel. They worked until the last minutes when dark fell upon the woods, and they went back home exhausted but excited. The next day would be much less hard work and much more exploration, moving in, and fun!

That night while he was asleep, Dace had a strange dream. He dreamed that down in the tunnel there was a little old man calling out for The Woodsmen.

The little old man said, "Come here, Woodsmen! Come here! I have an important message for you."

When the kids approached him in the tunnel, the man turned into a glowing ball of light that would go wherever they wanted to go throughout the tunnel. In this way, they were able to easily see their way through the normally-dark passages and explore deeper into the cave's winding, hidden tunnels. Just as Dace dreamed he was approaching some exciting new discovery, he awoke to the sound of his annoying alarm clock.

Dace jumped up and turned off the alarm, still thinking it would be neat if that strange, glowing little man would light up the tunnel for them as they explored. Today was going to be a big day, and The Woodsmen had no time to waste getting back into the woods!

Everyone met again, as usual, at Dace's house and set out on their journey. When they approached the crack near the rock face at the base of the cliff in the woods, they were shocked to see that only part of their bridge remained stacked there on the ground. Everything else they had stacked there the day before, including pieces of furniture and some gear, was gone!

Leila quickly resumed her command as official group leader and began to set up search parties. Jeff and Kevin were to stay next to the remaining bridge pieces and guard them. Nao and Van would search around in the nearby woods, and Leila and Dace would go inside the tunnel and see if someone had discovered their secret.

Cautiously, Dace and Leila approached the tunnel's entrance. Dace was about to speak when Leila quickly shushed him. They heard a scuffling sound coming from inside the tunnel! Was it a wild animal, or was it an intruder looking to steal more items from them?

The pair crouched down near the side of the tunnel entrance. The scuffling sound got louder. Whatever it was, it was coming closer!

Scrape, scrape, shuffle, shuffle. The sound got closer and closer. They could hear breathing now—heavy breathing. It definitely sounded like a person was about to come out of the tunnel. They were ready to confront the enemy and teach him or her a lesson. The scuffling and the breathing were almost there!

From out of the tunnel's mouth walked Anthony! He was breathing heavily and sweating a lot. He jumped back when he was startled by the sight of Dace and Leila crouching at the edge of the tunnel entrance.

"Anthony! What are you doing here?" Dace cried out in surprise and confusion. Anthony was supposed to be at his home a couple hours' drive away.

"Wow! You scared me there for a second. I wasn't expecting you guys for a little while longer, and I hoped I could get everything moved into the tunnel before you got here," Anthony replied, still panting from the heat and exertion.

"Why are you here? I mean, we're glad to see you, but I didn't even know you would be here!" Dace exclaimed.

"When I heard about all the work you guys had been doing and that you were about to go on another adventure in the woods, I just had to get back here and help. I begged my mom to talk to your mom, and, well, they worked things out where I can stay again for maybe two weeks!" Anthony said triumphantly.

Dace smiled, and simply said, "It's good to have you back, man."

Because Anthony had already dragged most of the gear, furniture, and bridge pieces into the main tunnel, the group was able to get to work immediately taking things into the left passageway. The fun was just beginning!

When all of the bridge pieces were stacked next to the cave pool in the left passageway, construction began. The two rafts were inflated so that no one had to get in the water during construction. All the pieces were slowly put together like a puzzle that spanned across the length of the water. As each piece was put into place, bolts were fastened to hold the pieces together. The bridge construction continued in that way until the final piece was in place and the bridge was one solid piece.

"I think Anthony should be the first to cross the bridge, in honor of his extra effort this morning and to welcome him back to our group—a group now of seven people!" Leila proclaimed.

Anthony blushed a bit, but he accepted the generous offer and led a cautious march across the new bridge. When everyone had crossed, they cheered and jumped around for a few moments. The bridge would open up a whole new area of exploration for the group, and it proved that they could build something truly useful for the tunnel. They were starting to feel like they could accomplish anything together.

Before they started exploring any more areas of the tunnel, the group decided to choose what rooms were for what. Bedroom-like rooms were scattered about the sides of the passageway. Many rooms had smooth areas for sitting, natural ledges for storing things, and even some cave formations that were like pieces of art. Between the entrance to the left passageway and the cave pool, the group counted eleven small rooms and two larger rooms. Each person got to pick a bedroom of his or her own from the small rooms. After seven of the small rooms were picked, it was decided that the remaining small rooms would be used for storage and the two big rooms would be used like meeting rooms or living rooms.

Most of the chairs and the table were placed into the first big room that the group decided to call the "living room." A few personal items were placed in some of the other small rooms, and the storage box that Dace and his dad had built was placed into a small room that was next to the living room. However, the group didn't put all of their gear into the storage box yet, because they were still going to need it for exploring that day.

After everything was in place, Van remembered the sign he had made. He said, "Hey, guys. We forgot to put the sign out front. I'm going to go put it out there now."

Van jogged through the passageway and out through the main tunnel entrance. Outside in the small clearing in front of the tunnel entrance, Van went to work as a small bird began to chirp nearby. He had the sign and a small metal pole to attach it to. First, he put some bolts through holes he had drilled in the sign and the pole. He fastened the bolts tight and then hammered the metal pole into the ground near the entrance. Like an ominous sign that underlined the "Beware of The Woodsmen" motto now posted, a small scorpion quickly scurried up the pole. Van shuddered at the sight of the scorpion, but he thought it fit perfectly with the dangerous mission that the kids had embarked upon. With the sign complete, The Woodsmen's lair would be marked forever!

When Van arrived back at the cave pool, Dace was there waiting for him. Dace looked excited.

"Come on! Everyone's starting to explore deeper into the passageway. Nao said it looks like the passageway curves to the right up ahead," Dace said to Van.

Dace and Van crossed the bridge over the cave pool while looking down into the perfectly-clear water below. The water looked like a refreshing swimming pool just waiting to be splashed and played in. However, that would have to wait for later. After a few minutes, they caught up with the rest of the group. Nao was continuing his hand-made map of the tunnel's passageways. The group followed the path curving off to the right and began to look around at all of the wonderful natural features of the cave. Looking at cave formations was kind of like looking at clouds because one could think up almost anything and find it in the gnarled rocks and sleek formations.

Some formations were colorful in the sense that they had multiple streaks of brown, white, and similar dull shades running throughout their lengths. Other formations had such odd shapes that the group thought they could see a hand, a foot, or even a dragon in the rocks. Of course, those shapes were simply part of their imaginations, but then something caught Kevin's eye.

"Hey, everybody, look over here!" cried Kevin.

Everyone ran over to where Kevin was crouching and stared down at the strangest little formation they had ever seen. Or was it a formation at all? In a hidden corner of the passageway, lying partially buried in the ground, there appeared to be a claw-like hand. The hand was very large; it was bigger than any hand or claw they had ever seen before. Anthony, who enjoyed studying about dino-saurs and ancient creatures, said he thought it might be a genuine fossil. This exciting news got everybody to looking around that area of the cave, searching for more fossils. Jeff noticed a small, strange-looking creature embedded into the cave wall, and Dace found a part of a bone protruding from the rock. They continued to look around, but they didn't find any other pieces of buried history in that area.

After a while, everyone decided to continue on through the passageway. As the passageway curved left and right, up and down, winding its way to somewhere, Nao suddenly exclaimed, "Stop! I think I know where we are!"

"How can you know that way down here?" asked Leila.

Nao answered, "Well, I'm not completely certain, but I've been mapping our progress, and..."

"And, what?" Leila pressed.

"I think that we are just about underneath Dace's house!" Nao replied excitedly.

"Cool!" Dace yelped. "I've always wondered what things were hidden deep beneath my house. I thought that, like, there could be dead people, ancient animals, and that sort of thing. I never knew there was a *tunnel* running right beneath my house! It's like having a subway running under your home. We have a secret passageway to travel right under our own neighborhood!"

The thought of such a secret passageway was exciting to everyone. Not all of the kids lived right in that neighborhood, but most of them lived nearby. They started to wonder what sort of things they could use a secret passageway for. They could deliver important, secret messages among the group. They could travel outside, in a way, without getting wet even when it was raining. Maybe they could even hide there if there were an attack from outer space!

Then Nao brought up the practical side of things. "It's really neat to have a secret passageway, but it's only really a secret passageway if we can get out of the other side. This part of the tunnel may not have an exit. For all we know, the tunnel may not have any exits, other than the entrance we came through."

What Nao said made sense, but the group still thought it was exciting to be standing underground underneath Dace's house or anybody's house for that matter. They decided to stop there and take a break to eat. Dace had the idea to make a little sign and attach it to the wall so that they would remember this spot. It would be like a street sign. Everybody started talking about naming parts of the tunnel like streets since they could travel through them just like roadways.

In between two curves was the straight area that went beneath Dace's house. The straight part was named "Hatch Street" after Dace's last name. The group also decided to make a sign for the first part of the left passageway where all of the rooms were located. They named it "Woodsmen Avenue." As they continued to walk a little farther down the passageway, it became rockier and steeper. In fact, the passageway started to go downwards very quickly. They decided to turn around and go back to Woodsmen Avenue and determine what to do next from there.

Back in the living room on Woodsmen Avenue, the gang was lounging around on their custom-made chairs and discussing the day's discoveries so far. A few of the group members wanted to get ropes and go back to the farthest point of the left passageway to continue exploring. A few others said they wanted to start exploring the other passageways that led away from the main tunnel. And still a few others wanted to stay right there in the living room and play some games. It had been another long, exhausting but fun day, and everyone finally agreed that playing some games sounded great.

During an action-packed round of Tower Break, Anthony had an idea. He told everyone he'd be back in a minute and disappeared somewhere off into the passageway. The fun games continued for a while, and Anthony eventually reappeared. He had a smirk on his face like something was up. The other kids were intrigued, and they followed him out into the passageway. There in the middle of the bridge sat two padded sticks.

Anthony said, "We can see who is knocked off the bridge and into the water first! Just get those padded sticks there, and we'll start playing."

Everybody loved playing water games, especially during the summer. Although it was cool down in the cave, just the thought of nearly triple-digit temperatures outside made the water seem even more fun and refreshing. Everyone splashed around in the water and got knocked off of the bridge numerous times. Some of the guys got an idea to shine the flashlights around, producing a strobe light effect. The water games were outrageous!

Once, when Nao had fallen deep into the water, he noticed something odd down near the bottom of the cave pool. Off to one side, there was a small opening, maybe just big enough for one person to fit through. He told everyone about it, and they all went down there to have a look. The opening appeared to be the beginning of a small water tunnel. With the right diving gear... Well, the group knew that diving, especially in caves, could be a very dangerous thing. They decided to forget about exploring *that* small tunnel for now.

It was starting to get late, and The Woodsmen knew they must always make it back home before dark. Luckily during the summer the sun shone for a long time. Evening seemed to last for hours and hours. They decided there was still a little time to explore before going back home for the day, so the group went back to the living room and decided what to do next.

"I have a great idea!" Dace yelled. "While Kevin is with us, why don't we have him go into the entrance to the middle tunnel and see what is back there? We can't see very far in because the passageway winds around to the right."

"Would you be willing to do that, Kevin?" Leila asked the boy. "We'd all be right there at the entrance, waiting for you and talking to you. We might even be able to use the walkie-talkies if you can go very far in. However, you'd have to go in alone since none of us are small enough to fit through the opening."

Kevin thought about it for a moment, and he had to admit that his first reaction was to say no. However, he realized that they might never get to explore that part of the tunnel if he didn't go in alone. In fact, everyone was counting on him to do the job. He would be a *real* Woodsman and be an important part of the group if he could do this. He decided to do it.

"Okay, I'll do it," Kevin said quickly before he could change his mind.

"Of course we'll give you a flashlight, a backup flashlight, and some other stuff to keep you safe. You'll be just fine," Dace told Kevin.

Everyone packed up their gear for the day and left out just the few items that Kevin would need to explore the middle passageway. They took one last look around at their handiwork down in the cave. They had multiple furnished rooms, chairs and a table, a real bridge crossing a natural swimming pool, and some storage for their gear so everything would stay neat and tidy. The tunnel was quickly becoming like a real neighborhood underground. The Woodsmen were both proud of their accomplishments and excited to continue exploring the cave. Their next task was to uncover the secrets of the middle passageway, and Kevin was the boy for the job. This would be another exciting adventure.

Chapter 9
The Hidden Jewel

After surveying their new home away from home, the group strolled leisurely back to the big passageway near the tunnel entrance. In the middle of the wall was a small hole, just big enough for Kevin to squeeze through. The hole was intimidating even though it was small. When one peered through the hole, there was only darkness. Even a flashlight only revealed a solid-rock wall and what appeared to be a small passageway curving off to the right. Kevin would truly be going into the unknown.

"Are you ready?" Leila asked Kevin.

"I guess," he replied.

"If you don't want to do it, that's okay. We can find another way to explore it later. We do only have about an hour or so before we have to leave for the day, anyway," Leila responded.

"No, I want to do this. I know I can do this," Kevin said with a determined look on his face.

Kevin gripped tightly onto his flashlight and made sure the small rope, extra flashlight, and walkie-talkie were secured to his belt. Then, without a long goodbye, he squeezed through the rocky opening and into the small passageway within. As he slowly made his way through the tube, following the twists and turns, he kept in contact with the rest of the group. He told them what it felt like to be in such an enclosed space all by himself. And, surprisingly, it was actually not that bad.

At first, the small passageway seemed rather safe, somehow. Kevin knew that nothing could approach him from behind since his friends were the only ones back there guarding the entrance. There didn't seem to be any side passageways connected to this one, so his only course was to crawl, climb, and squeeze his way forward. After a while, the walkie-talkie signal faded into static. He was alone.

Kevin was starting to feel like he had gone a long way in, and he thought maybe it was time to go back out. However, when he thought about turning around to go back (which would be hard to do in the tiny space), he had a nagging worry that something could follow him from behind. Some slimy little being could slither its way up from the dark tunnel ahead and silently creep along as Kevin crawled back out. Then, without warning, the creature could devour Kevin in an instant before the other kids could even know what was happening. Kevin started to get worried.

"Guys, I want to get out of here," Kevin suddenly whispered into the walkie-talkie, even though he didn't think they could hear him now. "I want to get out."

Surprisingly, Leila's reassuring voice cut through the static in short bursts. "Kevin, we can't get... (static) ...this little tunnel. You have to turn... (static) ...come back if you want to," Leila replied through the small device.

Suddenly the group heard a muffled scream echo through the middle passageway. It was Kevin!

"Are you all right, Kevin?" Leila asked worriedly into the walkie-talkie. There was no reply but the droning static.

Kevin thought he heard something up ahead, and he screamed. The noise from ahead sounded like hissing. What if it was a snake? Kevin started to panic, and he turned around in the passageway and madly clawed his way back through the winding tunnel. Most of the passageway required him to crawl because it was too short in most areas. He started to crawl quicker and quicker, and once he lost his grip and skinned his face on the rocks. He felt a small trickle of blood touch his lips, but he felt fine otherwise, so he continued to push his way onward toward the middle passageway's entrance. After a while, Kevin noticed that the hissing sound had stopped or was too far away to hear. He felt a little easier after that, since, even if it was a snake, it was obviously not near him anymore. He kept crawling until he made it back to the small tunnel's entrance.

Everyone was relieved when they saw Kevin approaching from within the small tube. Dace and Jeff helped pull Kevin out of the hole in the wall. Kevin felt a lot better to be out of that enclosed space, but he was starting to feel like he panicked too soon and let the group down.

"I'm sorry, guys. I guess I just got scared there for a minute. There was a really weird hissing sound. It just hissed and hissed, like a thousand snakes were slithering around in their hidden den," Kevin said. Everyone understood and didn't blame him for coming back out so quickly.

Nao suddenly had an idea. "Hey, Kevin. Was that passageway big enough for us to fit through?"

"Yeah, I think so, other than the entrance hole," Kevin replied.

"Well," continued Nao, "I think we could try to widen the hole big enough to where any of us could fit through it. Then we could find the source of that hissing. If it is a den of snakes, we really need to know. We might have to seal off this middle tunnel so that the snakes don't come this way."

Everyone agreed it was a good idea to check out just what was really hiding back in the middle passageway. The thought of thousands of poisonous snakes was scary, but they had to know the truth. So far, the group hadn't seen any animals in the cave other than small fish, and they had only seen a few bugs that seemed harmless enough. Maybe snakes were the real inhabitants of this cave. If Nao's plan to widen the hole worked, they would soon find out.

The group quickly headed out of the cave, chattering about snakes, secret passageways, and schemes on widening the hole into the middle passageway. It still wasn't dark yet, so the group decided to sit down in the clearing and build a small fire to roast chocolaty delights. There was always time for dessert!

As everyone sat around the fire and discussed their finds of the day, a dark streak darted out of the nearby bushes and ran across the clearing. It was Slasher! The bunny must have heard familiar voices and came by to check it out. Van—always ready to try something strange for a laugh—tried to get Slasher to eat a roasted marshmallow. Slasher seemed uninterested at first, but he finally took a small nibble. Dace joked that they were going to make Slasher fat, and they'd have to rename him "Slower" instead. The bunny didn't seem to laugh at that joke.

The crackle of the fire slowed and eventually dimmed to a small pile of red embers on the ground. Anthony and Van went to get some water from the stream so they could make sure the fire was out for good. It was getting late, and the group had yet another big adventure planned for the next day. Anthony and Van eventually got back with the water and drenched the embers. Everyone walked back to Dace's house while discussing the problem of widening the hole in the tunnel. Nao said he had an idea and that he'd work on it tomorrow. Everyone left Dace's house wondering what the next day would bring.

That night, Dace had another strange dream. The little glowing man appeared once again, but this time he beckoned Dace to crawl into the middle passageway. Dace somehow made his way in and followed the glowing man.

As they crawled along, Dace could hear hissing up ahead. The little man held a finger to his mouth as if to signal for quiet. Then he pointed up ahead. Dace could see a small glowing in the distance, as if another little glowing man was there waiting for them. He crawled forward and saw...

Screech! Screech! Screech! Dace nearly smashed his alarm clock that morning. He thought that he needed to get something less annoying. After smacking the snooze button two or three times, Dace finally got up. The group wasn't meeting as early that day, but Dace was riding his bike over to Nao's house and helping him bring some stuff back to Dace's. Nao wouldn't say what the things were, but he sounded pretty happy about it.

After an exciting bowl of cereal that tasted like tree bark (Dace's mom was going to the grocery store later that day to get some *real* food to eat), Dace set out on his bike. Dace loved roaming the neighborhood on his bike. The freedom of movement, the wind in his hair, and the exhilaration of going as fast as possible down the last hill before Nao's house were all some of the best things in the world. Dace often rode with friends, but he still rode alone whenever possible. Each bike ride was an adventure itself. Even though Dace had been down the roads in the neighborhood many times, he always noticed something new or thought of a fun game to play. Most often he pretended to be a secret agent searching for clues to an important case. Sometimes he pretended he was driving a race car, an old-time carriage, or some other type of extraordinary vehicle.

Dace went down into the ditch in front of Nao's house and popped up the other side. He skidded to a stop in front of the detached garage. Nao's house was an interesting place. Even though he lived in town in a fairly average neighborhood, the land had many trees, and the lot was larger than most. Nao's house was two stories and tucked in near the back of the lot. There was a huge front yard, very long and still surprisingly wide, but the backyard was tiny. A detached garage sat about thirty feet from the house, and a small bedroom was on top. The room was used as an office by Nao's dad, but there were a few years when Nao's parents rented the upstairs space out to someone.

The downstairs garage was where all of the action was happening. Nao's dad, Tom, had many tools, both hand-powered and electric, to build things. It was a hobby of his to make simple pieces of furniture and strange little gadgets. He was a tinkerer by nature.

As Dace approached Nao's garage, he heard a loud clanking sound. It sounded like Nao dropped a bunch of tools. Dace quickly ran inside to help.

"Ah, you've arrived!" Nao exclaimed with a smile. He seemed pleased with himself today. "I have a bunch of tools here that are going to help us widen that hole into the middle tunnel. I first thought of explosives, and that's what I tried to convince my dad to let me have. Unfortunately, I couldn't get them. I remembered that my dad has an old jackhammer out here that he used years ago to smash up some concrete when we were building a new deck out back. However, the jackhammer is electric, so we couldn't use that down in the cave without some sort of power source. Finally, I found these." Nao gestured to the ground where a pile of heavy tools lay.

There were numerous chisels, hammers, and grinding tools. They were all hand-powered of course. Dace was a little disappointed that the other ideas hadn't worked out. Chiseling away at solid rock would be pretty tough. However, they didn't have to make the hole very big—only a few extra inches—so he figured that seven people could actually get the job done in a reasonable amount of time.

Dace and Nao loaded up the tools into backpacks and started riding, somewhat clumsily, back toward Dace's house. During the ride back, Dace bumped his tire into the curb and went flying off of his bike. His hands and knees skidded across the pavement, and the heavy tools in his backpack slammed into him with a painful thud combined with metallic crashes.

"Are you okay, Dace?" Nao quickly asked as he jumped off of his bike and rushed to Dace's side.

Dace lay there a little dazed, but he was okay. Nao helped him get up, and they walked their bikes the rest of the way to Dace's house. Dace cleaned up his wounds and then prepared for the day's journey back into the woods. Today was the day they would explore the middle passageway!

Everyone arrived, and they set out into the woods. Leila said that she couldn't come out the next day, so everyone decided to get as much exploring done that day as possible and postpone their next adventure for a while. The group arrived at the entrance to the tunnel, and they smiled when they saw the welcoming sign out front. This place was starting to feel like home. Granted, it was a really big, winding home with secret passageways and dozens of unexplored areas potentially filled with snakes and deadly creatures. Still, it was like a home to the courageous Woodsmen.

The first task of the day was to start widening the hole into the middle passageway. Everyone put on protective eye goggles (and each of them, in turn, made fun of how funny the others looked in the goggles) and started chipping away. After a tedious period of time, Van told everyone to step back. He took a sledge hammer and smashed it as hard as he could onto a thin part of the rock. A big chunk of rock flew off into the hole as many small pieces scattered about onto the ground. It worked much better than they had expected.

Some of the guys took turns smashing at the edges of the rock for a while until some sharp pieces struck a few people, causing them to yelp with pain. Everyone decided to take a break and step back to look at their progress. The hole was wider on both sides now, and it was close to being big enough for everyone to squeeze through. For safety's sake, Nao suggested that they chisel off the sharp edges before crawling through the hole. After another thirty minutes of work, the entrance to the middle tunnel was newly widened and open for business.

"It's like we just widened a road or something. In a way, this is our second construction project in the cave," Dace said proudly.

"This was more like a *destruction* project, though," Van laughed.

Everyone realized the time had come to enter into the middle passage, and it was then that they remembered the hissing that Kevin had heard the day before. After all the adventures they had experienced in the woods this summer, the group wasn't about to be stopped by a strange noise. In fact, they remembered that they had found this very cave by hearing a noise in the woods. They still hadn't found any exits or passageways leading out of the cave to another part of the woods, but they knew that wind rushed into and out of the tunnels from somewhere, making that strange noise they first heard weeks ago.

"Who's going to go in first?" Dace queried. "We have to go single file because the tunnel is so small."

No one wanted to be the first to squeeze inside, and Leila was about to reluctantly volunteer since she was the group's leader, when Kevin spoke up.

"I'll go first," he said. "I was in there yesterday by myself, and I know I can do it again. I'll go first."

Some of the older kids felt a little sheepish that the youngest kid in the group was currently the bravest, but they let him go first anyway. After all, he knew more about this passageway than anyone else, didn't he?

Kevin crawled in. Next was Dace, followed by Nao and everyone else, ending with Leila. She figured if she wasn't at the head of the group, then she should be at the back in case they had to turn around. Crawling was a slow way to travel, and it hurt everyone's knees. Dace thought he should have brought the knee pads that he purchased after falling off of his bike last time. The group of seven took a long time to reach the point where Kevin had heard the hissing noise. They squeezed through large cracks in the rock, crawled beneath low ceilings, and attempted to walk in a few areas where the passageway was larger. When they finally heard the hissing noise, the group stopped.

"It sounds like it is coming from a million snakes!" Kevin screeched.

"Hey, wait a minute," Nao said. "That has a really smooth, consistent sound to it. Instead of snakes, it sounds more like steam or something."

The steam remark started off a flurry of conversations about dragons, volcanoes, and even a giant kettle boiling with water, just waiting for the kids to fall in. It was crazy talk. Confined spaces and the unknown put everybody on edge. They just knew they were close to discovering something big, whatever it was.

They continued forward. The passageway started sloping downward, and it eventually became so steep that they started sliding down it like a playground slide. It was a very bumpy, rocky playground slide, but still a slide. Kevin hit the end of the passageway first. Suddenly, six more bodies came bumping down the slide and squished him tighter and tighter against the wall.

Although the end of the small passageway seemed to be solid rock, it didn't sound very solid when Kevin first hit it. Nao noticed that fact and pulled out a few chisels and small hammers he had brought along in case they encountered any small openings or passageways slightly too narrow to pass through. He started chipping away at the hollow-sounding part of the rock in the dead-end passageway. Dace helped out with the other chisel. After a couple minutes they stopped chipping away. The air was so humid down there that the hard work made them breathe heavily very quickly. They were also starting to sweat a lot.

Way at the back of the group (for the passageway was still too narrow for everyone to sit next to each other even there at the dead end) Leila spoke up. "Hey, what is taking so long? Are we turning around to go back, or what?"

Nao shouted backward, "I think we found something interesting here! We're chipping away at the rock now, but it's pretty hard work."

Jeff and Van squeezed their way to the front of the line and took over chipping at the rock for a while. A small crack started to appear in the middle of the hollow-sounding area. This encouraged Jeff and Van to try harder. They started pounding away with the chisels harder than before. Suddenly, Jeff's arm went straight through the rock after a really hard hit on the chisel with the hammer. He nearly struck his head on the rock, but Van caught him first.

"Hey! I feel cool air down here through this hole!" Jeff yelled back to everyone else.

Jeff pulled his arm out of the small hole, and everyone felt a breeze of cool air drifting through the passageway. Then they noticed a soft glow coming through the small hole. Jeff bent over and peered through the opening in the rock. He sucked air inward with surprise. Everyone started asking him what he saw.

"It's amazing! I know where the hissing sound is coming from!"Jeff called out, overwhelmed by the sight.

Everyone else was prepared to hear about a giant den of snakes squirming around in a hidden cave pit, but Jeff surprised them all with his next statement.

"It... It's hard to see everything from this far back, but I think there is a waterfall down in there! And... And it is inside of a giant, cavernous room. There is a soft glow coming from somewhere—I can't tell where exactly. There also seems to be a lot of water everywhere," Jeff narrated what he saw as he continued to be awed by the sight. "I think we're high up near the top of the room. This passageway comes out probably near the top!"

Everyone was immediately concerned. What if the rocky end to the passageway suddenly broke and they all slid out, falling all the way down into that room? Who knows what could be waiting down there at the bottom! At the very least, the floor was probably rocky and dangerous. Nao, continuing his streak of ingenious ideas, thought of a way to make everyone safer.

"Quick—let's tie a rope to one of the solid formations back there and have everyone hang onto it," Nao said.

Anthony tied one end of a long rope to a solid-looking cave formation on the ground and tossed the rest of the rope forward and down to Nao. Everyone held onto the rope as a safety precaution, and Nao slipped the end of the rope through the small hole in the rock.

"What good is that going to do?" Jeff asked. "The hole is way too small for even Kevin to get through."

Nao replied, "I know, but that's about to change. Hang on tight, everybody!"

With that, Nao gave the rock near the hole a huge whack directly with his hammer. Everyone tensed up, ready for something to happen. Nothing happened.

Nao smacked the rock again, this time using the hammer against his largest chisel right near the edge of the hole. The small crack rapidly became a larger crack. Then the loudest creaking and cracking sound they'd ever heard exploded through the small passageway like gunfire. What happened next was a blur.

Even though everyone was holding onto the rope, a few rocks under Jeff's feet suddenly gave way. He quickly fell a short distance and almost lost his grip on the rope. Nao grabbed for him, and in turn, everyone behind him started grabbing onto the person both in front and behind them. There was now a human rope as well as the one made from fibers. Everyone was holding on tight, but they each knew they couldn't hold on much longer.

"Jeff!" Nao quickly yelled downward. "Does the rope go down far enough to reach the ground?"

Jeff yelled back, "I can't tell! There's a strange glowing light in this room, but the ground looks pitch black. It doesn't look like rock at all!"

Jeff let go of Nao's hand and starting inching his way down the rope to get a better look at the ground. After a tense minute of silence, the group heard a muffled splash below. In horror, Nao quickly tried to look down below to see if Jeff was all right.

Nao yelled toward Jeff, "Are you hurt? Can you hear me?"

There was no reply. Nao got a sick feeling in his stomach as he started to think of all the terrible possibilities. Jeff could be injured, or worse.

"Awesome! Guys, you *have* to see this! Get down here!" Jeff unexpectedly yelled up from the depths below.

Everyone could hear more splashing coming from Jeff's direction. It sounded like he was swimming!

"Okay, everyone, it sounds like it is fine down there. Let's start climbing down the rope. I want a second rope tied onto something else and tossed down there just in case this one comes off or breaks for any reason. We have to have a way back up," Nao stated with a commanding voice.

Leila tied the group's backup rope to another cave formation that seemed to be strong and tossed the rope down to the end of the passageway. Everyone started climbing down the ropes to the bottom of the huge, cavernous room.

A cavern was the best description of this hidden room. It was giant. The ceiling was more than fifty feet up from the floor, which was actually covered with water which the group was descending toward. The cavern room was extremely far across as well, but the group couldn't tell how far without more exploring. The room was also very beautiful. There were thousands of ceiling and floor cave formations—stalactites and stalagmites—and there was a beautiful, soft-green glow coming from the water. There was a tall waterfall off to the far side of the room, but the group couldn't tell where the water was going.

While the room didn't seem to be actively filling up with water, there was still a lake of the stuff across the entire bottom of the room. The water seemed to be very deep, much deeper than anyone dared try to descend, and there appeared to be an island in the middle of the lake. Off in the distance there was also a shoreline of sorts, made of solid rock. The walls and formations sparkled in the soft glow. With so much water dripping into this room, the cave formations were alive and healthy.

After the last person made it down into the water, everyone swam toward the island. The water was cool but not cold—it made for a pleasant swim. They eventually reached beach at the edge of the island and sat down to look at their surroundings. The glow was the first puzzling thing that needed attention. The water glowed everywhere and seemed to be alive. The Woodsmen hadn't had time to notice just what caused this glowing as they were busy with making their way safely to dry ground, but now they looked more closely at the water.

Everywhere in the water there appeared to be tiny, glowing creatures. The creatures zipped this way and that way through the water. Dace scooped a tiny creature into his hand and examined it more closely. It was about a quarter-inch long. It had little antenna, legs, and two small fins. It glowed softly with a greenish-tinted light, and upon closer inspection, it sometimes had other colors zipping around its edges in a wonderful, kaleidoscope-like pattern. It was indeed a strange-looking creature.

Dace carefully let the creature squirm back into the water, and he stood up to look around at the island. It was a rocky island with a fortress-like stack of huge rocks off to one side. There were cave formations on the ground here and there, and there was a rocky bowl of water in the middle. The small pool of water was only a couple feet deep and six or seven feet across. There were some sort of tiny, glowing fish swimming in the glassy pool. They appeared completely clear, and Dace could see the tiny bones and insides of the fish as they swam by. The fish were also very beautiful, just like the rest of the amazing cavern room. The ceiling soared high overhead and was covered with countless formations hanging down like icicles.

"Wow!" Anthony finally exclaimed after no one had said anything since arriving on the island. "This place is amazing."

Everyone agreed. The cavernous room was a hidden, glowing jewel deep within the cave. No one else knew this place existed. The Woodsmen had made their greatest discovery so far, and yet the upper tunnels of the cave still had so many more places to explore! The cave tunnels held many secrets for future adventures.

As they sat in awe in the middle of the cave island, someone checked the time. It was already three o'clock! How could the time have passed so quickly? They had been in the cave for almost three hours now. They had had to chip away at the entrance to the middle passageway, squeeze along its length, and discover a hidden cavern filled with glowing creatures. This had already been an exciting adventure, and there was more to come. There was much more to be explored and discovered that day.

Chapter 10
Secrets of the Tunnel

The Woodsmen explored the cave island further and found that it was about fifty or sixty feet across at the longest part. The island was shaped like a bean, and the tall stack of rocks sat off to one side in the thin part of the bean. Everyone looked closely at the ground for fossils, gems, or any treasures the island might have to offer.

After fifteen minutes or so of island exploration, Anthony called out to the group. "Hey, I found something over here!"

Everyone ran over to where Anthony was crouched on the ground, peering into something near the base of the towering, stacked rocks.

"It looks like another small passageway, but this one goes down—straight down through solid rock. It... It almost looks artificial!" Anthony said to the others.

In amazement, Dace and Nao kneeled down for a closer look. The opening did seem to be very smooth and round. It didn't look the same as all of the other rocky openings they had been through in the cave tunnels. It was also a straight path down. When Dace shined his light down, the boys still couldn't see the end of the pit. It could have been hundreds of feet, or it could have been just beyond the tip of the flashlight beam. Nao recommended that they drop a small rock down to see if they could hear it hit the bottom of the pit. Anthony tossed in a small rock, and after what seemed like minutes, they heard a small, metallic clank echo back up the pit.

"Metal?" Anthony asked in confusion. "Why would there be something metal down there?"

Nao replied, "Maybe it is a naturally-occurring metal ore deposit, like the ones they find when mining for gold, silver, copper—"

"Gold!" Anthony screeched. "We'll all be rich!"

Dace quickly cut in with a sensible thought, "I think we shouldn't guess as to what is down there since we can't reach it right now anyway. We'll only be disappointed if it's just an aluminum can or something."

"Yeah, but why would there be an aluminum can down there? I thought there were no signs of people having ever been in here before," Nao commented.

When everyone suddenly thought of the possibility of people having been there before, their muscles tensed. What if there were robbers who hid in this cave and stored their stolen goods down in that pit? What if someone was here now, watching them from a dark corner of the cavern? Could they really be safe down here? They all quickly agreed that they *had* to go into that pit and find out what was down there. It could be a matter of life or death!

The idea of going into a dark pit and feeling around for some unknown substance wasn't very appealing to any of The Woodsmen. They also had to figure out how to get down there today, before they were forced to take a break from the woods for a while. They just had to know now!

"I want to do it," Leila suddenly said. "I didn't go first when we were crawling through that tunnel up there, and I feel like I should take some more of the risks as group leader. I can't let everyone else always do the scary stuff."

"You've taken a lot of risks and shown bravery already!" Dace shot back.

"Yeah, I think you've been a great leader," Jeff said. "How about I go down there?"

Everyone suddenly wanted to go down into the pit themselves. They finally decided to play a game to determine who would go into the pit. Each person had to call out the name of a country, and everyone else had to guess its capital. Whoever got the most right answers would win the right to go into the pit and discover its secrets.

In a group of smart, educated kids, winning a trivia game wasn't easy because there were so many ties. After it came down to a tie between Leila and Nao, Dace had an idea for a tie breaker. Whoever swam over to the ropes and climbed up to the top first would win. The tie breaker had the dual purpose of determining who would go into the pit and also getting someone up to the top of the ropes because someone was going to have to stay up there and untie one of the ropes at the top. That rope would be used to descend into the pit, and the person who stayed up at the top of the small entrance into the cavern room would have to wait up there just in case he or she had to go back out and get more rope.

At the count of three, Leila and Nao dove into the cool water and swam furiously toward the dangling ropes in the distance. Schools of miniature, glowing creatures darted out of the way as the two competitors cut through the water. Both Leila and Nao were fast swimmers, but Leila's athletic build and competitive spirit ultimately won. She pulled ahead at the last moment and grabbed a rope. Before she could pull herself up the rope to the top, Nao called out for her to stop. He said that since it was obvious she would win, he would go ahead and climb carefully up to the top. It wasn't worth slipping and falling just to try to win at a game. She agreed.

Once Nao was safely up the rope and into the small passageway, he untied the longest rope and dropped it into the water below. He sat down at an odd angle near the mouth of the opening into the big room and waited for the results of the pit descent. He heard splashing down below as Leila dragged the rope through the water and over to the island. All alone up in his little tunnel seat, Nao couldn't help but daydream for a while. He relaxed and let his imagination drift freely.

Down on the island below, Anthony and Jeff were securing the rope safely to nearby rocks while Dace attempted to help Leila get ready for the descent into the pit.

"No, no, no! You're doing it all wrong!" Van finally said after watching Dace and Leila struggle with the rope for a few minutes. "It goes like this."

Van looped the rope around and tied it in fascinating ways so that it made a secure harness for Leila. Everyone was surprised by Van's knowledge of rope technique. He said that he learned it all from his dad, who was fond of camping and rock climbing. Learning knots and how to handle ropes properly was a great skill to have when exploring caves. Van promised to teach the group more techniques later so they would all be safer when using ropes.

Leila, properly secured with the rope, carefully stepped over the edge of the hole and began her descent into the pit. She carried the most powerful flashlight that the group had, but she couldn't yet see the bottom of the pit. She called out to the guys above to keep lowering her down slowly and she would let them know when to stop. As she descended, the air seemed to get cooler. It made sense since heat rises, but the cool air still gave her a chill. She examined the pit walls and was amazed at the beautiful, tiny fossils embedded in the walls. Most looked like fish and other small water creatures. There were also many shells. It was then that Leila realized that the pit was probably not artificial or man-made at all. It must have been steadily carved out by water, trickling down for countless years, slowly forming the smooth, pit-like tunnel going straight down.

The numerous water creatures must have lived in a vast, underground lake of sorts. Maybe the cave above was even filled completely with water during a time long ago. In any case, Leila was starting to feel more secure in thinking that no human had ever been in the cave before. She started guessing that the metallic sound below must have come from a natural deposit or something entirely different that simply sounded metallic but was not.

Leila continued her descent as she marveled at the fossils around her. At one point, she started feeling a slight draft of air, and she remembered that she hadn't looked down to try and see the bottom for a while now. She looked down and, surprised by the sight below, let out a small squeak. Up above, the guys heard the noise and called down to ask if everything was fine. They also wanted to know if she had found anything yet. Leila simply called back up for them to stop lowering the rope. She had successfully arrived at the bottom of the pit.

The bottom of the pit was very cool and slightly breezy. The ground was covered with smooth stones of various sizes. The ground was also slightly damp but not wet. Much water must have certainly been here once, but it was now simply a damp hole in the ground. Leila noticed these things quickly as her eyes darted around the bottom of the pit, taking in the sights. However, her gaze kept coming back to the strange object resting in the middle of the ground. It was shiny, definitely metallic-looking, and it didn't appear to be naturally occurring. The object was about one foot across and round. It had unreadable markings on the top and a symbol that looked like a square -shaped bird in the middle.

Leila bent down and picked up the object. It was pretty heavy and felt like metal. She examined it more closely, but there were no more features on the top that gave her a clue as to what it was. On the back of the object, there was simply a smooth, curved surface of the same metal as the top. She realized that finding a manmade object here at the bottom of the pit probably meant that *someone* was here at some point in the past. Although it could have also arrived at the bottom of the pit after flowing through the underground water streams and finally becoming lodged in the stones at the bottom of the pit. Regardless, Leila decided to untie herself, tie the object to the rope, and tell the guys to pull it up. They could examine it while she explored the passageway that she noticed off to one side of the pit.

Leila heard the guys above shriek with excitement when they brought up the object and saw its sleek, shiny exterior. She smiled to herself with satisfaction and continued on into the passageway leading up and away from the bottom of the pit. The passageway was cool and breezy just like the pit, and she thought she could hear outdoor noises in the distance. The rocky road slowly wound its way upward, meandering back and forth like a lazy river.

As Leila rounded a bend in the passageway, she saw light peeking in from far ahead. She quickly jogged up the last slight slope through the passageway until she came to a person-sized opening in the rock that led to the outside! She peered through the opening and saw that she was high up in the middle of a sheer cliff face looking down over the woods. She realized that this cave opening would be impossible to reach without ropes from above. She couldn't quite see what was up above at the top of the cliff, but it looked like more woods. This opening must be far away from Dace's house!

The midday sun streamed into the small opening, and Leila heard birds chirping and water trickling down a stream somewhere below. As far as she could see in the distance were trees and woods. Leila suddenly realized that the woods were much bigger than she first thought.

These woods must be huge, and The Woodsmen had a vast territory to explore! While she sat there admiring the woods, she temporarily forgot about the cave behind her and the guys back on the cave island who must be wondering where she was. She was so relaxed, so calm in the soothing sun and beautiful woods that she was inspired to write another poem.

Leila pulled out a small notepad and pen, and she wrote the following poem:

High over the woods in the afternoon sun,
I gaze upon future adventures and fun.
My mind meanders through soothing thoughts,
And my heart is warmed with adventuresome plots.
My companions and I will soon continue,
On to new paths of exploration and venues.
We are The Woodsmen, brave and sound,
And the woods will forever be our playground.

After finishing her poem, Leila remembered that the guys were probably wondering where she went. They didn't know that the passageway led to the outside, and she had to get back to tell them. However, it was so beautiful, so peaceful up there on the side of the cliff. Leila thought looking out over the woods was the best sight she had ever seen. She had to let the guys know what they were missing. She decided to put away the notebook and make her way back to the bottom of the pit inside the cave.

When Leila arrived back at the bottom of the pit, she called up to the guys to drop down the rope. No one replied. When Leila didn't hear voices above, she started to get worried. What happened to them? Where were they? Without the rope, Leila was stuck between the bottom of the pit and an opening on the side of a rocky cliff. She was trapped.

Leila started to get antsy after a few minutes, and she called up to the guys once more to make sure they hadn't heard her the first ten times. She was starting to panic, but just when Leila thought the guys had left her there forever, she heard Dace call down from above.

"Is that you, Leila?" he yelled down.

"Of course it's me! Who else would be down here?" Leila called back.

"Sorry! We were so excited about the object you sent up to us that everyone went up to Nao to show him. We got so absorbed into looking at it and trying to figure out what it was that we forgot you were still down in the passageway. Nao just remembered, and I volunteered to come down and get you," Dace said. He truly felt bad about leaving Leila down there even for just a few minutes. Oh, but that object! It was so fascinating. It looked like something from out of a movie. It seemed so ancient.

Leila replied, "Well, I guess I understand. But next time, leave the rope hanging down! I could have climbed back up with it instead of thinking I was going to die down here, a lonely explorer on the trail of discovery. Years later, someone would find my bones and wonder who had dared explore the dangerous cave. Then suddenly one of you Woodsmen would remember that you left me here years before! How would you feel then?"

Dace, feeling a little ashamed, sheepishly responded with, "I'm sorry, Leila. We just got so caught up with that thing. It won't happen again. And anyhow, you *have* to see what we found on it! Come on, I'll help pull you up!"

Dace lowered the rope and helped Leila ascend back up to the top of the pit. They both swam across the glowing cave lake and climbed up the rope to the small opening above. When they rejoined the group, Nao pointed out the tiny markings on the underside of the object. Kevin proudly announced that he was the one who had noticed the markings. However, in the dim light no one could read the tiny markings. They would have to wait until the group could make it back outside and get a magnifying glass.

After the group squeezed and crawled their way back up through the middle passageway in the tunnel, everyone climbed out into the front room where the three main passageways met. Everyone decided that they'd had enough exploring for one day, and they were exhausted anyway. They decided to go back out into the woods and talk about their adventures while playing near the stream.

On the journey out toward the stream, Leila told the group about her solo adventure through the passageway at the bottom of the pit. She described herself walking through the winding tunnel and seeing a light in the distance. Then she amazed everybody with her description of the cliff opening that overlooked the woods. Everyone was excited and eager to see the same view for themselves. They also wanted to find out just where in the woods that opening was. However, that would have to wait for another day and another adventure.

Crickets began to chirp, and the woods grew noticeably cooler. A summer's evening breeze drifted through the trees and rustled the underbrush. Evening was quickly approaching. The sounds of laughter and imagination filled the air as the seven kids played games. A lonely owl landed on a nearby tree and hooted once toward the group. Suddenly, everyone noticed how hungry they were and how late it was getting. The end was coming to a perfect summer adventure. The Woodsmen knew it was time to go home.

Chapter 11
Fall's Sweet Promise

The Woodsmen went their separate ways and continued to enjoy their summer vacations. Anthony stayed for a while longer at Dace's house, and the two boys devised another video game competition and party that they'd have near the end of summer. Nao spent a lot of time working in his garage, trying to create new things that would help The Woodsmen on their future adventures. The two brothers, Jeff and Kevin, went to a late summer camp and then to their grandparents' house to stay for a while. Leila had a busy summer schedule but still made time to meet with the boys for games every now and then. Van kept finding ways to play practical jokes on people, and he went camping in another part of the country with his dad. While camping, they panned for gold in a cold stream and fished for trout. Summer was moving along quickly for each of the brave Woodsmen.

Everyone in the group had a fun, full summer, but the end of summer was approaching quickly. After weeks of planning, everyone had agreed to meet a week before school started and have a big end-of-summer party. When the day for the party came, everyone met at Van's house. They were going to hold the party at Dace's, just like the beginning-of-summer party, but Dace's parents were going to be out of town that week.

Van's house was in the middle of the big city, about a twenty minute drive from most of the other kids' houses in the suburbs. Since Van lived near an awesome water park, everyone was going to go there for the first half of the day. They slid down towering water slides, rode on crazy rafts that dipped and bobbed in the water, floated in a giant wave pool, and finally relaxed on a lazy stream that slowly made its way around the entire water park.

That evening, everyone played games at Van's house and ate Super Cheese Guy's pizza. They also got to start a small fire in a fire pit that Van's parents had in their backyard. That night around the flickering fire, The Woodsmen listened to Van's dad, Mr. Steve Jonas, tell the scariest, most adventurous stories he knew. Mr. Jonas told of mythical creatures, scary adventures, and dark woods. The woods stories interested the group the most.

After the stories came to an end, the group sat there thinking silently for a moment. Strangely enough, many of the stories didn't seem so crazy after all the things The Woodsmen had been through together. They knew of dark, secret places that lay deep within the woods. They knew of hidden chambers, underground lakes, and glowing creatures lurking under the earth, waiting to be discovered. They knew of hawks circling high in the summer sky, gathering data to report back to their masters who hid in secret lairs. They even knew of ferocious bunny rabbits that stalked them through the woods!

There were many things that The Woodsmen knew about adventure, but above all, The Woodsmen knew of true friendship. They knew how they must stick together and help each other out in order to make each adventure a successful one. Each person was equal among The Woodsmen. Each one was trusted. Each one could be called the truest friend of friends. Each one truly knew of the bonds that forever tied them together as adventurers and friends.

The party ended, then summer ended, and school began another year. Weeks passed, and fall's sights, sounds, and smells seemed to fill the world with a different rhythm of life than summer. Summer had come with an exciting party and continued at a blinding speed with activities, exploration, and fun. It also went out with a blast as everyone celebrated the best summer yet.

Conversely, fall quietly crept up on The Woodsmen. Cool evenings became cool days, and trees changed their colors. Splashes of orange and red streaked through the woods, and leaves began to pile up on the ground. The beginning of fall meant, in many ways, the end of adventures for a while. However, the promise of fall was that the adventures were never truly over. Yes, winter would soon come along with snow and cold, but spring and then another summer were just around the corner. Fall was like the beginning of a restful nap that would last until spring aroused the sleeper to remind him that life was about to begin anew. The promise of adventure was never far away, and the tunnel lay there in its comfortable nook of the woods, waiting for the adventurers to return.

One quiet fall evening Dace was relaxing on a hammock outside. He was reading an adventure book and cheering for the adventurers to find the hidden treasures when suddenly he remembered a box at the back of his closet. The box contained a shiny treasure that The Woodsmen had found at the bottom of the pit in the cave. That treasure was a strange object with even stranger writings on it that none of the group could read. They had even forgotten about the tiny writing on the bottom of the object, and no one ever stopped to read it. At least no one had read it except for Dace when he remembered it a few weeks later. He was shocked by what the tiny writing suggested. He was surprised that he could actually read it. And someday—someday—he planned to tell the others what he had found. But that would be another adventure for another summer.

About the Author

Jesse Honn brings wit and a straightforward style of writing to readers who want to have fun, learn new things, and improve their lives. He has enjoyed writing for well over a decade but has only recently brought his skills as a writer to the public both online and in print. Although still young by some standards, Jesse brings experience to his writing as a former homeschooler, three-time college degree holder, father, and picky, dedicated observer of everyday life.

About Life Flight Media

Life Flight Media currently publishes informational and educational books and minibooks as well as fiction adventure books. Life Flight Media is interested in working with aspiring authors, musicians, and film producers on product promotion and distribution. Please contact us if you are interested in having Life Flight Media help you achieve your media production goals.

Life Flight Media has as its main goal the desire to inform and entertain people through innovative media products. We produce both niche, high-end products as well as products for the budget-minded. We will work with various media artists to deliver products tailored to a wide variety of tastes and interests. Here at Life Flight Media, life enrichment is what it's all about.